Moses Gaster

**Ilchester Lectures on Greeko-Slavonic Literature**

And its relations to the folk-lore of Europe during the middle ages; with two

appendices and plates

Moses Gaster

**Ilchester Lectures on Greeko-Slavonic Literature**
*And its relations to the folk-lore of Europe during the middle ages; with two appendices and plates*

ISBN/EAN: 9783337411589

Printed in Europe, USA, Canada, Australia, Japan

Cover: Foto ©Andreas Hilbeck / pixelio.de

More available books at **www.hansebooks.com**

# Greeko-Slavonic.

# ILCHESTER LECTURES

ON

# GREEKO-SLAVONIC LITERATURE

AND ITS RELATION TO

*THE FOLK-LORE OF EUROPE DURING THE*
*MIDDLE AGES.*

With two Appendices and Plates.

BY

M. GASTER, Ph.D.

LONDON:
TRÜBNER & CO., LUDGATE HILL.
1887.

**Ballantyne Press**
BALLANTYNE, HANSON AND CO.
EDINBURGH AND LONDON

# PREFACE.

*The purpose of these Ilchester Lectures, delivered at Oxford in the spring of 1886, is to show, on a small scale, the importance of the Slavonic literature in the literary history of modern Europe, and likewise to call attention to the vast materials, hitherto untouched, which are preserved in the literature and folk-lore of the Slavonic nations.*

*In treating of the religious and popular literature, I confined myself to the most important texts and immediate sources. My references to authorities it would be very easy greatly to increase.*

*In another work, however, I contemplate the publication of all the Slavonic texts belonging to the apocryphal literature, in the form of an English translation, with copious notes and introductions.*

*In two appendices I have traced both the origin and history of the "Bible Historiale" and of the Glagolitic Alphabet from a wholly new point of view.*

*Finally, I take great pleasure in expressing my heartiest thanks to the Trustees of the Ilchester Fund for honouring me with the invitation to deliver these lectures at the far-famed University of Oxford. I value the honour all the more, as I had just arrived in England, an exile, banished by the Government from my native country of Roumania.*

*I wish also especially to thank Mr. I. Abrahams, who kindly assisted me in reading the proofs.*

M. GASTER.

London, March 1887.

# CONTENTS.

# VII.

---

# APPENDIX A.

# APPENDIX B.

# I.

INTRODUCTION: VARIOUS THEORIES OF THE
ORIGIN OF FOLK-LORE. — THE GREEKO-
SLAVONIC LITERATURE.

A

# I.

To watch the rise of new nationalities or of new literatures is, without doubt, one of the most interesting spectacles; it is to see before one's eyes scattered elements being built up into a living organism, with all the marks of a characteristic individuality. Such a process of development is often presented to our gaze, though at a distance, when we seek to follow out the progress which one or other branch of culture has made in order to arrive at the form in which we at present have them,—as, for example, the origin of language, of writing, of civilisation. The same problem which such questions offer is likewise presented to us by the rise of any literature, in so far as it throws light on the modern poetic constructions of civilised nations. The question whether it is mechanical mixture or organic assimilation meets us at the very outset. Hence the investigation of sources is a characteristic of our critical age. We are chiefly interested in finding out what are the elements which the literary artist finds given to him, and which he proceeds to organise into a higher unity.

What is the part played by the unconscious poetic activity of the people? what that of the conscious art of the poet? Nay, we must proceed farther, and raise the question, which has hitherto been considered unnecessary: How far have the people any creative imaginative power? Do the peoples create independently of one another poetic products derived immediately from the influence of surrounding Nature? And how far can we assume this creative impulse in modern times?

The investigations which we include under the name of *Folk-lore* have had their beginning quite recently, and have, therefore, undergone considerable modifications and changes. It is the merit of the Romantic school in Germany, which arose at the end of the preceding century, to have directed attention to the hitherto neglected literature of the common people. Herder was the first to collect the folk-songs of many nations. Clemens and Brentano made collections of the German folk-songs, as Bishop Percy had done in his " Reliques of Ancient English Poetry." Thence they turned to other products of the popular imagination, especially to the fairy tales, then the sagas and legends, proverbs, riddles, and superstitions. First in these investigations, both in time and importance, were the brothers Grimm, to whom Germany owes so much. Hand in hand with the collection went the exploration of the popular literature, which had thus passed from the nursery and the chimney-corner into the study of the scholar. Grimm, the creator of German mythology, is likewise the founder of the school which we may term the *Mythological*. According to this school, traces of the archaic Northern mythology have been preserved in the fairy tales and in the whole of folk-lore. The old gods and goddesses, dislodged from their thrones, have still survived in the form of demons, ghosts, elves, dwarfs, &c. ; and the remarkable similarity of the fairy tales of all nations is explained on the assumption that their mythologies were originally identical.

By means of investigations into the Vedas, especially at the hands of Kuhn, a view of the ancient mythology was taken up which regards it as an incorporation of natural phenomena. The names of these phenomena, *Dyaus*, *Varuna*, &c., were accepted as gods and worshipped. Thus many mythological words have been shown to be metaphorical expressions for the sun, the moon, the clouds, and the rain. This having been shown for Hindu mythology, the method was then applied to Greek and Northern mythology, although the circumstances were here quite different ; for among the Greek divinities were to be found many not of Aryan origin, as *Aphrodite* the Syrian *Militta* (= Moledta, the generatrix), or *Herakles* the Phœnician *Melkart*. The problem is still more

difficult in the case of the Northern mythology,
which is of comparatively much later date, at
any rate as regards its appearance in a written
form. The fairy tales being now only obscure
relics of the mythology, they must be explicable
in the same manner, and must likewise be explained as sun, moon, and cloud myths. So, too,
all the superstitions, customs, and generally the
whole popular thought in all its manifold mani-
festations. All these, so far as they could not
be connected with the dogmatical religion, were
referred to the same mythological origin. Then,
according to this view, the poets absorbed it from
the people and developed it. This is the most
wide-spread and most popular view of the origin
of folk-lore, especially that of Europe.

To this I append another theory, which, from
a chronological point of view, is the latest, but the
principle of which is closely connected with the
former. The most outspoken representative of
this theory is Mr. A. Lang. He also considers
fairy tales and customs as an ancient inheritance
of every nation, further maintaining that they
are nearly related to the mythology. So far this
theory goes hand in hand with the Mythological;
but the difference between the two is, that, according to this view, which I term *Prehistorical*, both
myths and fairy tales as well as customs, are not
the outcome of etymological speculations and the

embodiment of natural phenomena, but the relics of a primitive state of savagery.

The proofs adduced in support of this *Prehistorical* theory are analogies and comparisons with similar, or what are presumed to be similar, tales and beliefs current among primitive tribes and uncultured nations of the far East. This analogy between them is thus explained as the result of a similar intellectual development, where the one retained the primitive form better and clearer than the other, and these tales are only like the flint-stone chips covered by a later stratum of culture.

But in the same way as our modern philology does not allow us to compare directly French or English with Sanskrit or Zend, but retraces step by step the history of their evolution, in the same way can we not compare our tales and customs directly with those belonging to a tribe far distant in time and in space, of which we neither know the age nor the connection, where many links in the chain are missing, if there is a chain at all.

This theory rests, then, like the Mythological, upon the presumption that all that we call now-a-days folk-lore is of hoar antiquity, and the genuine property of every nation. Both will be, therefore, shaken to their foundations if we succeed by a closer inquiry to prove that it is often the result of a long development; that it is relatively modern, and that the similarity between the European and the primitive and tribal folk-lore is a deceptive one, or ought to be explained in quite another way.

Indeed, the Mythological theory, and in this way the Prehistorical too, received a severe blow from another, which I term the *Theory of Migration.*

Benfey, in his celebrated introduction to the *Pantchatantra*, applied first this theory to the greatest part of European folk-tales, tracing them to their Oriental origin and proving their comparatively recent date. They passed, as he shows, from nation to nation, very often *in written form*, and from this passed to the people, among whom they were assimilated more and more to the peculiarities of each nation. The same contents received a different and a national form.*

The folk-tales have now no longer claim to be considered as mythological, and the influence to which they owed their origin was quite the opposite of this. For the most part, they became the common property of the European nations through *literary transmission.* This has been proved, further, for many modern fairy tales. Thus Boccaccio's tale of "Griseldis" has been followed till it became a fairy tale. Thus, too, the story of Genevieve, ori-

---

* In a remarkable essay Professor Max Müller has carried out the same line of thought, and has shown the travels of an Eastern tale through a number of literatures, till it reached Lafontaine, and followed its traces step by step till the story becomes more and more Europeanised and nationalised.

ginally a miracle of the Holy Virgin, has likewise become a fairy tale. Examples of this might be easily multiplied, showing clearly the influence of written literature on oral tradition.

Proceeding a step farther, we may apply this theory of migration, or better, this *Historical* theory, not only to the fairy tales to which it was confined, but also to the other branches of popular literature, like sagas, legends, adventures, and superstitions, and finally to the Northern mythology itself. Cannot the foreign and literary origin of this be proved? Are all those marvellous tales and fabulous beings originally European? Is the naïve poetic world of the common folk filled with superstitions, creeds, and legends regarding the most unnatural and unexpected events as the most ordinary things in the world, the remainder and residue of an old, forgotten mythology, and of a more ancient state of savagery? or have they been brought on the crest of a mighty wave of culture to the furthermost shores of Europe, and thus form *one stratum* in all the peoples of Europe? Can we not in this way explain their similarity to one another?

The very advance of our spiritual and imaginative life hides from us any direct vision of this development. Much has been destroyed, and we must deal with the remainder as with a palimpsest. We have to take in hand some decomposing principle which shall remove the more recent writing

and enable us to decipher the faded relics of the
older signs.  But that which eludes our grasp in
the West of Europe is offered to us in rich pro-
fusion by the East, especially the South-East, with
its own peculiar culture.  The Greeko-Slavic world
has remained in nearly the same condition as
Europe was when it was ruled solely by *Christian* thought and by *Christian* civilisation alone.
While the West has advanced farther, the Greeko-
Slavic world has remained at this point, and accordingly its literature is to us of peculiar interest, as
it enables us to observe accurately the process
by which a written literature, generally of foreign
origin, influences oral folk-literature.  We see the
alien element accepted and assimilated, the popular
imagination gradually enriched.  We can then observe the reaction of this latter on poetic genius,
which takes in the feelings and thoughts of the
people, and expresses them in elevated and elevat-
ing artistic form.

   I term the body of literature with which I contemplate dealing the *Greeko-Slavonic*, because it
is confined to works translated from the Greek into
Slavic tongues, and where we have, therefore, the
*literary sources* beyond any doubt.

   Bulgaria, as we shall see in the short historical
sketch with which I conclude this work, was, after a
struggle for centuries, incorporated into Byzantium,
and the influence of Greek, already great, became

the sole influence for two centuries. The whole
literature was modelled after the Greek, and even
later, after independence had been secured under the
Asenides, Greek retained much of its power. Thus
arose the literature which we term for this reason
*Greeko-Slavonic.*

This literature is not only that of the Bulgarians,
but is also the Church literature of the Servians,
Croatians, Roumanians, and Russians ; and it began
early to spread over these lands. The Old Slavonian
tongue in which it is written has remained the holy
or Church language of these lands up to the present
day, except in Roumania, where it was superseded
in the seventeenth century by the vernacular.
Thus this literature, together with the Greek,
offers the counterpart of the Latin civilisation,
favoured in a far higher degree, as this was, by
social and political circumstances.

Besides the interest which this literature affords
us, as I have sketched out above, as regards folk-
lore and the history of civilisation, it also gives
material of no small critical worth for dealing with
Greek, and especially Middle Greek literature.
Many a work of the Byzantine period has been
preserved for us in an improved form because it
was early translated into Slavonic. Modern science,
both in profane and in ecclesiastical history, has
begun to make use of these Slavonic texts for critical
purposes as yet only in a sporadic manner, as

both the extent of this literature and its language
have prevented access to foreign investigators.

I select from the whole field of Greeko-Slavonic
literature, not the dogmatical, but rather that portion which shows a *living course of development*,
and brings before our eyes an example of the process by which the spiritual wealth of a people is
increased. By this means the clue will be given us
to many an imaginative product which we meet
with in folk-lore, and which we have hitherto regarded as the peculiar property of the people, or as
the survival of earlier mythological conceptions.
Investigation into these matters is only in its
infancy, and we have first to settle the facts, if we
do not wish to lose ourselves in the field of vague
hypotheses. It is, therefore, the heretical and
poetical literature that will engage our attention,
likewise derived from the Greek, yet powerfully
influencing not alone the Bulgarians, but also all
the other nations who came in contact with the
Old Slavonian language and literature. Many
traces will be seen in the mediæval literature of
Western Europe, and I hope to be able to prove
that *the religious literature* was the most important
factor in this branch of the development of European civilisation, and that the influence of the Old
Slavonian literature was just as important and decisive towards the West as it was towards the East.
The results at which we shall arrive will accordingly

permit of an application to the whole literature of the Middle Ages, in which many points will appear under an entirely new light.

The fantastic and imaginative apocryphal literature, the romances and epics, the didactic fables, were touched by wide religious movements in Bulgaria, and have exercised a deep influence on the imagination of the nations. Folk-lore arose out of a *written* literature, whose traces we meet with in saga and romance, in religious and epic poems, in riddles and tales, and even in popular beliefs, customs, and habits. In the following pages I shall attempt to sketch this literature in a brief outline, devoting the greatest attention to the most conspicuous points, as well as to those least known in Western Europe. Within the circle of our investigations we shall thus include the Apocrypha of the Old and New Testament, the literature of history, legend, and amulets, and lastly, the literature of the fable, as it was transformed from literature into folk-lore.

# II.

## THE BOGOMILISM; ITS SPREAD AND INFLU-ENCE. — THE APOCRYPHA OF THE OLD TESTAMENT.

# II.

## THE BOGOMILISM; ITS SPREAD AND INFLU-ENCE. — THE APOCRYPHA OF THE OLD TESTAMENT.

## II.

AT the same time with the culmination of the Bulgarian power and the Bulgarian literature (which
I shall portray at the end of these lectures) began
a powerful religious movement, which was accompanied by results of far-reaching consequence. I
refer to the heretical movement known under the
name of *Bogomilism,* which ruled Bulgaria for not
less than five centuries, and left indelible traces in
the spiritual life of the Slavonic nations.

A more thorough - going investigation of this
movement in its spread throughout Europe leads
us to still more astonishing results. We come
across traces of it everywhere, and a good part
of the religious literature which later on became
folk-literature may be traced back to the influence of these heretical sects. Even the romances
of chivalry, when divested of their trappings, show
themselves as Oriental tales that have found their
way (always a long way, and often a dark one)
through many intermediaries to the place where
they are now found.

As this view of mine is more or less novel, I will
permit myself to enter into it in some detail. This

B

is the more permissible as we are dealing at the
same time with the earliest and least altered literary
remains of the Slavonic literature upon which I am
called to lecture, and these form besides the greater
part of it.

At the time of the conversion of the Bulgarians to
Christianity, there were to be found at the Bulgarian
court ambassadors or missionaries from the Paulicians or Manichæans of Asia Minor. In addition
to these there were a number of Jews, who had also
come to convert the people to their belief, while
they were still hesitating about Christianity. The
Paulicians had settled in Thrace at an earlier date.
The Emperor Constantine Copronymos transported
a large number of them in the eighth century from
Asia Minor, and thus at the same time transplanted
the seed of Manichæism in the modified form introduced by Constantine of Samosata. The success of
these Paulicians, as they termed themselves, was
very great, and in the tenth century they had there
six churches. This religious movement attained
to particular importance through the appearance of
the priest (Popa) Jeremiah (c. 940), who called himself *Bogo-mil*, i.e., *Theo-philus*, like the disciple of
St. Paul. After him his followers termed themselves *Bogomili*, and Bogomilism kept a foremost
place in the history of the Balkan peninsula for
many centuries. In Bulgaria itself it became so
powerful in a short time, that councils were fre-

quently assembled at Sofia to oppose its heresies.
But all these efforts were in vain. Bogomilism had
taken too deep a root in the heart of the people;
its power could not be destroyed. This movement
spread even farther. Thrace became the cradle of
an analogous movement throughout Europe. The
apostles of Bogomilism carried their creed first to
the coast of the Adriatic, then to Italy, whence the
movement spread to Germany and Southern France,
and even as far as England, where at Oxford in the
twelfth century a council was summoned by Henry
II. to take steps to eradicate a new kind of heresy
which had made its appearance in London and
York. Under different names we find practically
the same heretical sects from the tenth to the thirteenth century in the following places:—In Bulgaria, Macedonia, and even on the Black Sea, and
in Russia towards the east: in the West, in Italy,
especially in Lombardy, Mantua, Verona, Treviso,
Bergamo, Milan, Piacenza, Ferrara, Bologna, Faenza,
and Orvieto; in France, throughout the south, but
also in Paris, Orleans, Rheims, and Brittany; and
in Belgium and Holland, and over the whole basin
of the Rhine—Metz, Strassburg, Cologne, Bonn,
Triers, and Goslar. We have already referred to
England.* It is clear that this movement was a
lasting one, and could not have been without en-
during influence.

* Wesselofsky, Solomon i Kitovras, St. Petersburg, 1872, p. 142 *seq.*

These sectarians called themselves simply "Good People," "Good Christians," "Christian Poor ;" by others they were named *Bogomils, Manichæans, Paulicians, Patarenes* in Italy, *Kathars* in France and Germany (whence the German *Ketzer*), and likewise Bulgarians (whence the French *Boulgres, Bougre*). All this shows that they everywhere retained relations with their spiritual fatherland, and that the leaders of the movement in Bulgaria were recognised by them as authorities. Thus, in the year 1167, Nikita, the bishop of the Bogomils of Constantinople, issued a summons for a council of the French *Kathars* to be held in Toulouse.

A survey of their doctrines also shows the same unity of belief among them. Their fundamental principle was Oriental dualism as developed by Mani. It is still undecided whether and how far Buddhist influences were also at work. This world they regarded as the work of *Satanael, i.e.,* of Satan-God, who is a fallen angel. The misery of this world is therefore his work, as he fights against the good and tries to destroy everything. But redemption had come with Christ ; the Old Covenant, which Adam had made with Satanael, had been broken by Christ. But only the Bogomils or Kathars (*i.e.,* Pure Ones) are the true followers of His teaching, and man could only attain to holiness by entering their communion, and by this means he could save his soul from

farther transmigration through human bodies;
for *metempsychosis* formed part of their belief.
They therefore laid upon themselves all kinds of
mortifications, and their leaders and old men lived
as ascetics.  On the other hand, they threw over
the doctrines of the dominant Church, based their
faith more upon the Holy Writ, excluded the
cross from their religious symbols, and advocated
freedom from the domination of the Catholic
Church and of the nobility.  Eschatology formed
also a favourite topic of theirs—the theory of the
Last Things.  Thus the two extremes of creation
and destruction, beginning and end, cosmogony
and eschatology, the fall and the redemption,
formed the chief subjects of their thought, and
likewise the chief contents of their preaching.

Their views about an evil principle found ready
acceptance among the serfs, while their antagonis-
tic attitude towards the Church and the nobility
made them acceptable to the opponents of both
institutions.  If we add that they propagated their
doctrines chiefly and solely in the vernacular languages, and that they clothed their views in the
guise of fantastic and poetic tales, we can then
form some idea of the deep impression their doctrines must have made.  This is confirmed by
history when it speaks of a crusade against the
Albigenses and of one against the Bosnian heretics,
to which the whole of Christendom had to be

summoned by the Pope. And yet it was not
completely stamped out; we find an echo of the
movement in the Flagellants and the Hussites.
Europe had been shaken to its very depths by the
Crusades just before, and by this means the soil
had been prepared for this new heretical movement.

Now in the literature of this period we notice
a remarkable transformation. The old epic songs
of the cycle of Charlemagne gave way to new
poems filled with adventure and imagination; songs
and sagas free from the fetters of space and time
make their appearance; a whole cycle of popular
religious literature arises. Can all this be accidental and without any relation to the heretical
movement? Hitherto investigators, with but few
exceptions, have not thought of any connection
between the two.

But a careful examination of the chief elements
of their origin shows us that in most of them we
have only the disguised figures of other well-
known pieces. Merlin and Arthur, as well as
Marculph and Saturn, are no other than Solomon
and Asmodeus. In the saga of the Holy Grail we
have echoes of Oriental tales. And more; the same
influence is found in folk-songs and in popular
manners and customs. The mediæval belief in
Satan, with its outcome, witchcraft, as we shudder
to see it in the protocols of the Inquisition, is the

child of the dualism of the Kathars and Bogomils. Here we find the rule of Satanael on earth as a kind of counterpart of the rule of God in heaven. It was but a short step to worship him, so as to obtain favour with him, or, on the other hand, to make amulets as a protection against his power.

The literary activity of the Bogomils was indeed by no means slight. Popa Jeremiah himself is said to have written much, *e.g.*, the "Legend of the Cross," "How Christ became Pope," &c. But the chief use was made of the Apocryphal writings, which were translated from the Greek, or rather revised in a sense corresponding to their wishes.

They were even very well read in the Holy Scriptures, and at one time their bishop in Bulgaria boasted that there was not a *single one* among his 4000 disciples who did not know the Scriptures by heart. Now it is a very remarkable fact that the earliest translations of the Bible into the vernacular languages, especially into French and Italian, were not made from the Latin Vulgate, but without doubt from the Greek, or from one of the translations derived from it. In all probability they came from the Kathars, and were possibly translated from the Slavonian. And, in fact, we can easily explain this; for every religious reform begins with the study of the Bible; and again, these sects could only influence the common people by means of the vernacular. We may now go a step farther, and ask what kind of Bible was it which they used? Did they confine themselves to the simple translation of the text, or did they rather adorn and amplify it so as to suit their views and to make it more pleasant and accessible to the people whom they wished to convert?

From the earliest times, as soon as the Bible had become the Book, κατ' ἐξοχην, the source of all faith and knowledge, the naïve readers could not remain satisfied with its plain contents, often incomplete, and at times seemingly contradictory. Many of its stories were too short, many names merely mentioned in the Bible : on these points pious curiosity needed to be satisfied. The reader would ask : How did Adam plough the earth, for he could have no knowledge of that art? How did Cain know about death, and how did his parents bury Abel, for previously there had been neither death nor burial? Again, what is meant by saying that God took Enoch? What was the punishment of Cain? Who was Melchisedek, and why was he called a priest? Such questions could be asked *ad infinitum.* As a consequence, a number of legends arose already in earliest times, intended to fill these lacunæ and find answers to all these questions. These form the *Apocryphal Literature,* which only became of practical importance when it was adapted by heretical sects to their own needs. These tales were often of a poetic cast,

derived from the popular taste and glowing imagination, which made them most suitable for a wide
circulation among the people. The heretics altered
various points in them in agreement with the
views which they professed. And since these
Apocrypha were represented as the work of Biblical
personages, the doctrines and sayings put in their
mouths gained additional influence. For this
reason the Apocrypha were particularly favoured
by all sects, whereas the Orthodox Church often
condemned them, as in the well-known *Decreta
Gelasii*, the lists of Athanasius and Nicephorus.

It is thus by no means surprising that we find
the greater part of these Apocrypha in the Old
Slavonian literature of the Bogomils, and for the
most part with very slight alterations, which in-
creases their value for critical purposes. Some of
these are even attributed to Popa Jeremiah himself,
among them the "Legend of the Cross," as I
have already mentioned. As we shall see, however, he merely altered older Apocrypha to accord
with his views.

The original sources of this literature, which travelled through Europe and left permanent traces
of its influence on literature, poetry, painting, and
sculpture, are Greek texts, which came to Constantinople from the East and passed on thence to
the Bogomils. A second source, equally Oriental in
its origin, was supplied by Jewish legends, found in

the Haggadical writings, and in particular in a book called *Sepher Hayashar*. This book, which has the title of a work quoted in the Bible (Joshua x. 13), is a kind of *Biblical history*, wherein Genesis and Exodus are completed by numerous ancient legends, which are mostly incorporated without alteration. Thus the Biblical history becomes a Biblical romance; truth and fiction are inextricably mixed, and form together a complete Bible adapted to pious readers. It did not, however, prevent separate sections existing in independent form—as, for example, the story of Abraham and Nimrod, the struggles of the sons of Jacob with the inhabitants of Palestine, the legends of the birth and death of Moses, &c., &c.

Precisely the same thing we have before us in the Old Slavonian literature of the Bogomils. We have special Apocryphal writings attributed to various personages; we have also—though this has been hitherto unknown—an Old Slavonian Bible-story, in which all these legends form one whole, and which enjoyed enormous popularity and wide-spread circulation. This Bible-story, called *Palæa* (*i.e.*, Παλαία Διαθήκη), may have been originally copied from a Greek model, but in its existent and perhaps extended form it contains several legends which are almost literally translated from the *Sepher Hayashar*. This *Palæa* belongs probably to the tenth century, and is thus several centuries older than the corresponding works in Germany and France. These are independent of Comestor's work *Historia Scholastica*, which, as I may incidentally remark, usurped later on the name of the *Biblia Historiale.* The *Speculum Historiale* of St. Vincent of Beauvais is likewise a kind of Bible-story. Neither of these have hitherto been satisfactorily traced to their origin. It is only natural to assume that, like the earliest translations of the Bible, these Bible-stories may have been derived from the heretical sects, especially as these Bible-stories would find an even easier access to the people owing to their legendary and poetic form. It is, of course, also possible that they were afterwards revised and freed from their heretical elements. A few traces of these still remain, *e.g.*, a cosmogony varying in order and in details from that of Genesis. Other details confirming this view must be here omitted, as I devote a special chapter to a more close inquiry into the origin and the sources of these Bible-histories.* I must content myself here with these short hints and revert to the story Bible as it appears in Slavonic literature.

As I have already remarked, this contains a number of Old Testament Apocrypha, to which it is confined. Instead of going through them all, I will select some of them of special importance for their wide-spread or deep influence, and follow

* Appendix A.

these through the stages of their development till
they become part and parcel of the popular mind.
I reserve the Apocrypha of the New Testament for
the next chapter, as they present peculiar features,
and form a transition to the literature of amulets.

Looking to the cosmogony,* we find that it
presents an unusual form. On the first day God
created heaven and earth; on the second, sun,
moon, and stars; on the third, paradise; on the
fourth, the sea; on the fifth, birds and beasts; on
the sixth, Adam; and on the seventh God breathed
into him the breath of life. It is, as it were, a
counterpart of St. Basil's *Hexaëmeron*, which
attempted to explain the creation according to
the Bible. The fallen angels then occupy a large
space, but I must here pass them over, as they do
not offer anything special, and the legend never
existed as a separate Apocryphon.

Of still greater length and of far wider importance are the legends which deal with the creation
of man, his fall, repentance, and death. The
mind of Christendom has always laid great weight
upon all this, in order to reach its scheme of
redemption, to which everything in the Biblical
stories had to refer, as the goal of human fate.
Beginning and end of the process had to be combined, and the pious required a prophetic glimpse
of the final redemption while dealing with the

* Tihonravov, Pamjatniki otrečennoi russkoi literatury, St. Petersburg,
Moscau, 1863, ii. p. 443 *seq.*

beginning of sin. This association of ideas, per-
ceiving in the Biblical history a religious drama,
where the restoration of the fallen humanity is
foreshadowed in the Old Testament and fulfilled in
the New Testament, is an essential characteristic of
this heretical literature, to which I will revert,
and which I hope will give us the key for the
origin of the mediæval *Biblia Historiale*, and in
connection with it the "Bible of the Poor."
Hence the extent and number of apocryphal
tales dealing with this episode. These received
various names, such as *Historia Adæ et Evæ*, or
the "Legend of the Cross," or the "Pilgrimage of
Seth to Heaven." In Slavonic we have, in the
first place, the creation of man told in the favourite
form of question and answer, as we find it frequently in the Middle Ages, especially in the so-
called *Lucidarius*. In a fifteenth-century copy of
this Slavonic text* we read as follows:—

" *Question.* What holds up the earth ?

" *Answer.* The water.

" *Question.* And what the water ?

" *Answer.* A mighty rock.

" *Question.* And what the mighty rock ?

" *Answer.* Four golden fishes (whales).

" *Question.* And what the fishes ?

" *Answer.* A stream of fire.

" *Question.* And what holds the fire ?

* Tihonravov, 1.l.

"*Answer.* A fire double as hot.

"*Question.* And what holds up this fire ?

"*Answer.* An iron tree, which was the first thing created, and its roots are supported by God."

Then comes the cosmogony, which we have given, only it is in the form of question and answer, which continue as follows :—

"*Question.* How did God create Adam ?

"*Answer.* Out of eight things: earth, sea, stone, wind, sun, thought, the speed of the angels, and finally from the Holy Ghost."

This is made clearer in another MS. of the same age. "The body is made out of earth, the blood from the sea, the eyes from the sun, the thoughts from the clouds, the bones of stone, the breath from the wind, fertility from fire, and the living spirit out of God Himself." *

Both of these accounts have now-a-days become the common property of the people among all the Slavonic nations. These as well as the Roumanians repeat them in their songs, creeds, and in their religious ideas, and I might quote innumerable examples if I dared linger over this point. Even to the present day the people explain an earthquake as a movement of the fish on which the earth rests. Even in the popular recitations at Roumanian weddings the origin of man is described exactly in the same way as the above.

* Pypin, Očerku literaturnoi istorii starinyhu povêstei, St. Petersburg, 1858, p. 140.

The tree on which the earth stands is of Oriental origin, and occurs again in Northern mythology in the form of the *Ygdrasil.* There we find a parallel account of the creation of man, but in inverted order: the giant *Ymir* creates the world out of his own limbs, the sea out of his own blood, the mountains out of his bones, the rocks out of his teeth, the heavens out of his skull, the clouds out of his humour, and the trees out of his hair.* A corresponding cosmogony is to be found among the Manichæans,† according to whom the world was created out of the first man, the *Urmensch* of the Germans, the *Adam Kadmon* of the Jews. It also occurs in popular Russian literature, in the celebrated *Golubinaya Kniga,* in which the most heterogeneous elements have been combined into an epic whole, and which may be regarded as the outcome of a whole cycle of apocryphal stories. I will therefore give it complete in a literal translation at the end of the treatment of the apocryphal literature.

After Adam and Eve had been created by God, they were tempted by Satan in the form of a snake with a woman's head; they fell into sin, and were driven out of Paradise. All this, together with their repentance and their contract with Satan, forms the so-called "Confession of Eve"

* Grimm, Germ. Mythology, ed. iv., p. 464 *seq.*
† Flügel, Mani, p. 87 *seq.*, and the annotations.

(*Ispovedanye Evyne*), which is also an introduction
to the "Legend of the Cross," and indeed represents
a peculiar treatment of it. Its contents are plainly
dualistic, which settles its origin without difficulty.
Slightly condensed, it runs as follows : *—

"Eve tells her children that when God had
created everything, all things stood under her rule,
and no beast dared to touch her. But then came
the Devil in the form of a bright angel and tried to
seduce her. She repulsed him, and then came the
serpent as a bright angel and offered her the forbidden fruit. She trusted in the serpent, as favoured
by God, and ate, and gave some to Adam. Immediately the leaves fell from all the trees except the
fig-tree. Then God drove them from Paradise. The
Archangel Ioil interceded for Adam and Eve in
vain. They stood for a fortnight before the gates
of Paradise, and then had to leave in order to find
something to eat, but they found only thistles. So
they returned to Paradise, and Adam complained
of the good fortune which he had lost, and begged
God to give him at least a flower as a remembrance
of it. God therefore sent to him incense (*ladan* and
*liban*). At their further request, God sent them
the Archangel Ioil, and he gave them the seventh
part of Paradise for them to work in ; at the same
time he sent all the animals out of Paradise, and
gave them to Adam. Adam, however, had scarcely

* Gaster, Literatura populara romana, Bucuresti, 1883, p. 271 *seq.*

begun to plough the earth, when Satan appeared
and said, 'The earth is mine: Paradise and
heaven belong to God. If you are willing to become mine, you may till the earth; but if you
wish to belong to God, go back to Paradise.'
Adam answered, 'The earth and the heavens are
God's.' The Devil said, 'Give me a written agreement that you are my property, and I will leave
you.' And Adam said, 'I and my children belong to Him whose is the earth.' Thereupon the
Devil rejoiced, and broke a stone and wrote this
upon it. (Another variant makes Adam place his
hand upon it, leaving a trace of it on the stone.)
The Devil preserved this stone in the Jordan, and
placed four hundred devils to guard it. When the
Saviour came, He placed Himself on this stone
when He was baptized in the Jordan, and broke
it, so that the agreement between Adam and the
Devil was at an end.

"Adam now went before the gates of Paradise
and cried and mourned; at last he determined to
do penance. Eve went to the river Tigris and
stood in it forty days; nevertheless the Devil tried
to deceive her twice, once in the form of an angel,
the other time in that of Adam. After the forty
days Adam came himself, who had done penance in
the Jordan, and removed her; thus they were both
freed from the Devil. Many years passed by;
Adam became ill; his children assembled around

c

them and asked them what was the matter, for
they had never before seen anybody ill. Eve said
that he had a longing for the fruits of Paradise,
and that this was the cause of his illness. Thereupon Seth determined to go to Paradise and bring
something thence to satisfy his father. He came
there, and obtained from the angel a branch of the
tree of which they had eaten. Adam recognised
the tree, drew a deep sigh, and waved the branch
round his head and died. Three angels with
lights came to bury him. After these angels had
prayed for a long time, God received the soul of
Adam graciously. Adam was then buried by Seth
in the spot called *Gherusia Plata.* A voice called
out to Adam, ' Remember what I said to you :
Earth thou art, and unto earth thou shalt return.' The voice called out to the earth, ' It
is thine, and was formed from thee : to thee all
things return.' And Eve died six days after.
Out of Adam's head a huge tree grew."

The source of this narrative is the so-called
*Apocalypse of Moses ;* * but this does not contain
the characteristic point of the contract between
Adam and Satan, in which the dualistic principle
is clearly expressed. *Every single episode* of this
tale occurs again in varied form in popular literature. The complaint of Adam is everywhere repeated wherever this story reached—in Bulgaria,

---

* Tischendorf, Apocalypses Apocryphæ, Leipzig, 1866, pp. 1-32.

Servia, Roumania, and Russia. Curiously enough, the contract survived in nearly literal form in most of the reproductions. A part of these popular songs became *star-songs*, or, as they are called in England, *Christmas carols*. Iconography also made use of the legend, and Russian pilgrims often refer to the stone on which Christ stood at His baptism.

In close connection with this legend stands the " Legend of the Cross," one of the most wide-spread and celebrated of the Middle Ages. It is found in Latin MSS. of the twelfth century, and finds a place in Provençal, Italian, German, and English literature. The legend in its simplest form is part of the apocryphal Gospel of Nicodemus, and it has often been versified. References to it are to be found in Dante. It was made the subject of a poem by Gottfried and Viterbo, and of a drama by Calderon. It is, of course, accepted by the Bogomils, and attributed to Popa Jeremiah, their founder. In Old Slavonic it is still extant in two forms, of which one is by Gregorius Theologus, the other by a certain Severian Gavalski. I will here give the version which comes nearest to the original Bogomilist form, and is more extensive than the parallels of Western Europe. In the Old Slavonian version the history of all the three crosses is given, whereas in the West only that of the Saviour is dealt with. Brought into proper order,* the legend runs as follows :—

* *Cf.* Wesselofsky, Razyskanija, St. Petersburg, 1883, x. pp. 367–424.

"When God created the world, only He and
*Satanael* were in existence. The latter stole some
of all the seeds which God sowed in the earth, and
planted them in Paradise. Thereupon God drove
him out of Paradise, and Satanael became black.
From the seeds he had planted rose a mighty tree
with three branches; one belonging to Adam, the
other to Eve, and the third to God. At the Fall,
Adam's branch fell into the Tigris, and was taken
out therefrom; Eve's was carried by the Flood to a
place called Merra. After the death of Adam, Seth
kindled a perpetual fire in his memory by the side
of the tree, and placed wild beasts to guard it.
When Lot sinned, Abraham set him as a penance
to bring three logs from the tree, to plant them and
tend them with water, which he should bring in
his mouth. His sin would be forgiven when the
logs had grown. They grew into a mighty tree.
Moses took the second root, and with it made sweet
the bitter waters of Marah. Both the trees were
brought to Jerusalem by King Solomon to be used
in the building of the Temple, but they could not
be adapted to that purpose. At times they were
too short, at times too long. On one of them Queen
*Sivila* (*i.e.*, of Sheba) sate and burnt herself, whereupon the trees were hidden in the Temple. It was
on these trees that the two thieves were crucified,
the good thief on Lot's, and the wicked one on
Eve's.

"Now Seth had brought a branch of the third tree to his father, who made himself a crown out of it, in which he was buried. Out of this grew a wonderful tree, with three trunks that yet formed but one. This tree was brought by the demons to Solomon, who by this means obtained possession of Adam's skull, which was in the roots of the tree. This was so huge that a servant of Solomon once took refuge in it from a storm. Solomon ordered the skull to be brought to Jerusalem, and to be stoned. This was the origin of the place called *Lithostroton* (also Golgotha). This tree also was of no use for building purposes, and was taken up. It became the Cross of the Saviour. When Christ was crucified on it, His blood fell through the rock upon the head lying beneath, thus freeing Adam from sin, and redeeming him."

This is the Slavonic form of the legend, and there can be no doubt as to how it arose. The mention of *Satanael* alone would prove its heretical origin, and still more the whole line of thought, so far as it is preserved after the orthodox revision that it has undergone. It is only from the standpoint of Bogomilism, which rejected the cross, that we can explain the planting of it being attributed to *Satanael*, or the trait that the demons brought it to Jerusalem.

Of the other episodes I will only linger over that relating to Lot, which reminds us of Aaron's rod, and which, in the form of a symbol of repentance, has spread so far. Who does not remember the saga of Tannhäuser, or the innumerable Slavonic, Roumanian, German, and French legends in which the blossoming tree is a sign of sin and forgiveness?* Still more numerous are the legends in which the appearance of blossoms on dead branches is mentioned, though these are undoubtedly derived from the Biblical story. Among others, I may mention a saga about Charlemagne, which is preserved in Turpin's Chronicle. Saints innumerable have performed the same miracle, and even the beginning of Bohemian history is connected with a similar miracle.

I must pass over other apocryphal stories, and can only refer to the rich embellishment which the stories of Cain, Lamech, Noah, and others received. Melchisedek, who is specially mentioned in the New Testament, is represented by three Apocrypha, which aim at explaining his omission of the name of his parents and his character as "priest of God." The best known is that translated from the Greek of Athanasius, which represents him meeting Abraham in the beginning and being selected as priest by the latter.

A favourite theme was the life of Abraham, his destruction of the idols of Nineveh, his contest with Nimrod, and so on up to his death. With

* Gaster, *l. c.*

regard to the last topic, we have in Slavonic literature an Apocryphon which, so far as is at present
known, has not been found in Greek, though there
can be no doubt that it originally existed in that
language. It is there described how Abraham was
taken up into heaven, and saw there the judgment of men after death ; he returns to earth, and
struggles against death with all his might. Death
appears to him in an attractive form, and finally
deceives him into drinking his cup of poison.
Founded on an earlier Oriental legend dealing
with the death of Moses, this Apocryphon forms a
model of a whole series of similar imaginative
products portraying the struggle between man
and death, and the final victory of the latter.
Almost all literatures present examples of this,
especially in the form of folk-songs. In modern
Greek, the conflict of the hero *Aniketos* (Russian,
*Anika-voyn*) or *Digenis Akritas* with Charon and
with death forms the subject of such songs. I
may also remind you of the *danses macabres* of
the Middle Ages, of Titian's celebrated picture,
&c. The counterpart of this, the flight of the
hero to the land of the immortals, is an equally
wide-spread theme from Ireland to India. But we
cannot linger here, nor even on the Testaments of
the twelve sons of Jacob (of which we have a
Slavonic translation of the fourteenth century, of importance for the criticism of the Greek text), nor at

the minor legends about Moses, but must pass on
at once to the legends about Solomon, which are of
such importance in the history of literature.

The Biblical accounts of the wisdom and riches
of Solomon, the visit of the Queen of Sheba, the
building of the Temple, and so on, caused him, even
in early times, to be made the hero of. a whole
cycle of legends, round which other stories and
legends, derived from various sources, crystallised.
These in their turn underwent so many changes
in their wanderings towards Europe, that it often
requires a special investigation before we can
recognise the original legend in its latest form. I
will draw attention to two of the episodes, because
one of them had great influence on Russian epic
poetry, and the other is connected with the saga
of Merlin and with Bertoldo. Let us begin with
the latter.*          ·

"In order to build the Temple, Solomon tried
to get *Kitovras* (*i.e.*, Kentauros), the chief of the
demons, into his power. His general seized Kitovras, bound him with a chain, on the links of
which the name of God was written, and brought
him to Jerusalem. They went straight on, but as
they would have destroyed the house of a widow if
they had continued to do so, Kitovras broke one of
his ribs in two in order to avoid it. He heard a man
asking for shoes which should last seven years ; he

* Wesselofsky, Solom. i Kitovras, p. 209 *seq.*

burst out laughing. He sees a prophet ; he laughs
again. He sees a wedding; he weeps. Finally,
he guides a drunkard the right way. When
brought before Solomon, he casts at his feet a rod
four feet in length. He explains to Solomon that
the bird *Nogot* possesses the worm *Shamir*, by
which stones can be split without the aid of iron,
the use of which was forbidden in the Temple.
He then explained what had happened. He had
laughed at the buyer of shoes, because he had only
seven days to live. The prophet stood over a
treasure, and promised good luck to other people
when he could not tell his own. The newly
married bride would die in three days ; and the
drunkard was a just man, of whom it was said in
heaven that he was worthy of protection. The
rod gave the length of the grave which would
receive Solomon at his death, though he was now
so ambitious of power."

This remarkable tale is originally Talmudical,
where the demon is called *Ashmedai*, here Kitovras,
from the Greek *Kentauros*. The story occurs in
a German form under the name of *Solomon and
Markolph*, and develops into a mere dialogue
between a king and a sharp-witted but vulgar
man. Between the two we have the saga of
Merlin, in which Merlin plays the part of Ashmedai-
Kitovras; for he is brought before King Arthur,
goes through the same exploits on the way, and

explains them during the interview.* We have,
further, the dialogue between *Ben Sira* and *Nebu-
kadnezar*, and in a later form, in Anglo-Latin,
a dialogue between Saturn and Marolph, and a
still later development in *Bertoldo*, the well-known
Italian chapbook.

Still more like a romance is the other specifically
Slavonic story of *Solomon and Kitovras* or *Solomon
and Por*. This runs as follows :—Kitovras hears of
the beauty of Solomon's wife, and sends a magician
to bewitch her. He succeeds, and brings her to
Kitovras. Solomon comes in disguise, after he had
arrayed his army dressed in three uniforms before
the city. His wife recognises him and delivers
him up to Kitovras, who orders him to be hanged.
Solomon begs as a last favour that the trumpets
be blown three times, as he is a king. At this
signal his army advances in its battalions, red,
white, and black (explained by Solomon as fire,
clouds, and devils). They kill Kitovras and his
people, and likewise the faithless wife. This tale,
either in whole or in part, has passed almost literally
into all the popular literatures of these peoples,
and out of it stories and tales, and especially epic
songs, have been made. I mention only Roland,
who blows *three times* his trumpet, &c.

Less important are the legends of the destruction
of Jerusalem and the seventy years' sleep of *Abed-*

* Ellis, Early English Metrical Romances, ed. Halliwell, 1848, p. 31 *seq.*

*melekh.* He afterwards receives Jeremiah when he returns from exile with his people ; Jeremiah, seeing a heavenly vision, announces the coming of the Messiah, whereupon he is stoned by the people. The story, which is only to be found in Slavonic, modern Greek, Roumanian, and Æthiopic, seems also to be one of the old apocryphal legends, 'which have hitherto been regarded as lost.

Finally, we may refer to the legend of the Babylonian kingdom, in which a king orders the image of a dragon to be placed on all objects. As a punishment God causes all these dragons to spring into life and devour the people, while round the city an immense snake coiled itself. There is the grave of *Shadrach, Meshach,* and *Abednego,* and thence the messenger of the Emperor Leo brings a crown sent by these saints.* That Babylon was the home of dragons and basilisks was a wide-spread belief during the Middle Ages, and of this I might adduce many examples. I mention here only Sir John Mandeville.

Out of all these and other smaller elements was compiled the Slavonic Bible-story, which exercised so important an influence on the popular imagination.

* Wesselofsky, Archiv f. Slav. Philologie, ii. 1, 2, and Zamétki, St. Petersburg, 1883, i. pp. 9–14.

# III.

*THE APOCRYPHA OF THE NEW TESTAMENT.—ANTI-CHRIST.—LIVES OF THE SAINTS.—THE LETTER FROM HEAVEN AND THE FLAGELLANTS.—THE "GOLUBINAYA KNIGA."*

# III.

Pious curiosity, that is, the wish to fill up the lacunæ presented by the Biblical relations, was also the principal cause that led to the origination of the Apocrypha of the New Testament, especially the writings commonly known as Apocryphal Gospels.

As Mr. Cowper says in his introduction to the English translation, " Men were curious to know more than the Canonical Gospels contained. Fragmentary stories or traditions were abroad relating to Joseph and Mary and their families, to the birth and infancy, the trial and crucifixion of Jesus, to Pilate, Joseph of Arimathea, Nicodemus, and so on. How pleasant if all these fragments could be rendered complete, and especially if the silence of the four Gospels could be supplemented! The wish was not a barren one, and from time to time writings appeared professing to supply the information which was wanted. Some of these writings may be considered introductory to the evangelical narratives, others as appendices, but all as supplementary in one way or another. Joseph and Mary were no longer the obscure individuals the Gospels have left them ; the incarnation, birth,

and early life of Jesus no more remained imper-
fectly recorded ; the last days of Christ's earthly
life were set forth with wondrous minuteness of
detail ; the space between the death and resurrection of the Saviour was filled up with particulars
of what happened in the unseen world, as well as
at Jerusalem and elsewhere. Pilate was pursued
into every nook and corner; all he did and said
was noted down, and the steps of the Nemesis
which hunted him beyond the very grave were
diligently traced."

No question that these writings were largely
used by heretical sects, which sought support from
Apostolical or Divine authorities. So we find a
Gospel ascribed to Nicodemus, another even to
Marcian, the head of the *Gnostics,* &c. These
books were used to support various doctrines and
opinions concerning Christ, Mary, the resurrection,
and so forth.

The Apocrypha of the New Testament make
indeed their appearance very early in Slavonic
literature, as well as elsewhere, but under somewhat different circumstances to those of the Old
Testament. While the latter were more or less
inserted into the actual text of the Bible, the other
Apocrypha found no place in the actual text of the
body of the New Testament, and had, as it were,
an independent existence. This fact is connected
with the circumstance that the Bogomils, as well

as at an earlier date the Gnostics and Manichæans, were opposed more or less to the Old Testament. Its only value was as an announcement and prepara- tion for the New Testament. Interpolations and expansions were therefore permitted in the former. Their relation to the New Testament was quite different, since it was the foundation of their creed, and as such enjoyed special sanctity. It did not, however, prevent numerous legends of Christ, of the Holy Virgin, and of the Apostles to be circulated and modified in accordance with the desires and views of the heretics. On the contrary, the holy character attributed to this pseudo-epigraphical literature raised its value and made it fitting for the propagation of those views.

As is well known, the Apostle John, the author of the Apocalypse, which answered so well to their system, was the Beloved Apostle of the Bogomils, and many a book and revelation is ascribed to him. The Gospel of St. John was especially worshipped, and we will see farther on another book containing the fundamental belief of the Bogomils ascribed also to St. John. Incidentally I will mention here the Knights Templars and the Knights of St. John, both later accused of heresy, as well as the Freemasons, who all took their oath on the Gospel of St. John and had a special feast of St. John. The German *Johannisminne* may also be brought into connection with this, being till now not satisfactorily explained.

D

The Bogomils attributed, further, a number of apocryphal tales to the Apostle Paul, as well as to the Holy Virgin, or, better, accepted and changed them.

A peculiarity of nearly all these was that they dealt with eschatological questions. While the Old Testament, as enlarged by the means I have described, answered the inquiring or curious minds with regard to the creation of the world, of man, or the origin of evil, the Apocrypha of the New Testament solved the problem of the fate of man after death, and thus completed the drama of redemption. These writings included descriptions of heaven and hell, and gave instructions how to reach the former or how to avoid the eternal fires of the latter.

There is now a great difference between the Apocrypha of the New Testament and those of the Old, especially as regards those with which I am dealing. The Apocrypha of the Old Testament gradually make their way among the people, but in the process often lose their name. Their contents are preserved, episodes out of them are freely modified, and they thus pass, as it were, into the very blood of the people. Being assimilated by the people, they form a basis for further poetic expression, while the Apocrypha of the New Testament, attributed to holy personages, who are actually worshipped and form a part of the religious creed,

are preserved, with slight alterations, in a distinct
book form. They are never incorporated into the
body of the Holy Scriptures, but have themselves
their own *holiness*. The very names given to them
endow them with a kind of sanctity.

Of greater popularity, and of greater importance
for the literature and civilisation of the world is
the "Gospel of Nicodemus," especially through its
legend of the cross, already mentioned, and above all
by the "Descent of Christ to Hell," which is there
described by two eye-witnesses from hell. We have
presented to us the approach of the Saviour, the
bursting open of the gates of hell, and the liberation
of all souls, from Adam downwards. It also contains wonderful details of the trial of Christ before
Pilate and of His passion. There is scarcely a
European language into which this Gospel has not
been translated. The Latin translations are very
early, and were inserted by Jacobus a Voragine
in his *Historia Lombardica*, or "Golden Legend," a name of which Longfellow made use. It
does not come within our scope to follow the
work through all the literatures of the world. I
will content myself with referring to the Anglo-
Saxon translation which was printed at Oxford in
1698, though this had been preceded by an English
one in 1507. The well-known "Passion plays"
are based on this Gospel, and the influence of its
"Descent to Hell" is proved by the many imita-

tions, including those of Dante and St. Patrick. It
is true that classical literature had its " Descents to
Hades," but at the time when this literature appears
the influence of the classical models may well be
doubted. Many references in Dante show clearly
that he was acquainted with the " Gospel of Nicodemus." In Slavonic literature, besides the text
itself, we have many reminiscences of it among the
popular literature. The " Descent to Hell" itself
gave rise to a remarkable imitation, " The Descent
of the Holy Virgin," and it is easy to imagine the
influence it would have on the popular fancy,
especially as it was from the beginning regarded
as the clue to the mysterious life after death, and
therefore gave an opportunity of entering into all
possible torments, while the original Gospel only
spoke of a place of wailing and gnashing of teeth.
It is not at all surprising that we meet with this
in versified form when the popular songs deal with
man's soul after death. In Roumania it plays a
great part in the so-called wakes for the dead, i.e.,
in the songs sung by the side of the corpse.

On the other hand, the story has become quite a
popular and largely circulated book, and is called
also " Letter of the Mother of God," as a parallel
and counterpart to another " Letter of God " Himself, both of which I shall shortly examine.

In close connection with the " Descent to Hell "
is another apocryphal writing attributed to St. Paul,

which is likewise of great antiquity. This deals particularly with the condition of the soul at the moment of death, with the severance of the soul from the earth, and with the way it must go to reach heaven or hell. This too was a theme likely to rouse curiosity, and its treatment would be welcome to pious believers.

The first support for the contrast between the deaths of the righteous and the unrighteous is to be found in the Bible, where it is said, "It came to pass that the beggar died, and was carried by angels into Abraham's bosom." This was repeated about innumerable saints, as St. Barbara, St. Paul the Hermit, &c. But the clear contrast between righteous and unrighteous is to be found in a remarkable manner in the writings of Mani, the founder of the sect of Manichæans, who has a special chapter on the point, almost in exactly the same words.* The same picture is frequently repeated in religious and mystical tracts, in burial and other sermons, and in other moral writings intended to influence the imagination of men by this means. We thus find it even at the present day in folk-books, as in the so-called "Mirror of Human Life" in French.†

Especially noteworthy are, further, the *stations* or posts through which the soul has to pass before it reaches heaven. These are guarded by the demons

---

* *Cf.* Flügel, Mani, pp. 100-101.     † Nisard, ii. 29.

of human passions, which demand their rights from
the soul. This idea arose first in Egypt, it occurs in
the "Book of Enoch," &c., and the early Fathers of
the Church concerned themselves greatly with this
question. We meet with it also among the Manichæans, and very often among the moral writings
intended for popular reading. Several visions of the
saints repeat it, St. Macarius and others, that of St.
Basil the younger at the greatest length. The idea
took root in popular songs, and especially in popular
superstitions: songs at wakes wish that the departed
may come safely through the "stations" of heaven.
Many ceremonies connected with burial may be
traced back to these tales of the fate of man after
death. Most remarkable of all, this description,
combined with that of hell, has given the material
for the Russian block-book of the last judgment of
the world. A careful comparison between picture
and tale brings out clearly the connection of the two.
This may be traced farther back, as the Russian was
originally South Slavonic or Byzantine, and served
as frescoes in church. The picture is rightly to be
called "The Last Judgment of the Soul after Death :
its Reward and Punishment," for this is all of the
last judgment to be found in it.

I have perhaps lingered too long over this Apocalypse, and must pass on to the legend in which the
same Macarius plays the principal part, namely, his
journey to Paradise. This was a harder task. The

Apostle Paul, it is true, saw Paradise in his Apocalypse, but he speaks little of it. It seems as if only
the sorrows of men can make eloquent and can be
depicted, but not their happiness ; so he tells very
little about this, and what little he does say failed
to find its way into the mind of the people. Others
sought to find Paradise, but they only saw it from
afar, and could not come near to it. This was the
case with Alexander of Macedon in the *Alexandreis*,
and this too happened to St. Macarius, whose apocryphal tale is entirely taken from the work of Pseudo-
Callisthenes. Happiness is not granted to man in
this life !

Among those questions which have moved men's
souls, and still move them, is then the question of
the *end of all things.* When and how will the end
of the world come? It is true the Apocalypse of
St. John had given an answer to this, and depicted
in glowing colours the approach of Antichrist, the
signs of the world's end, and the last judgment.

It is sufficiently well known how these thoughts
interested not alone the Christian, but also the
Jewish and Pagan worlds. This description of the
burning up of the world is especially emphasised
in the religion of Zoroaster. We meet with it too
in Mani, as well as in Teutonic mythology, where
it plays a principal part. I do not, of course,
propose to pursue these ideas farther. I will
content myself with remarking that St. Jerome

has a similar description of the signs which are to precede the last judgment. So, too, the Venerable Bede, and after him a crowd of ecclesiastical writers.

The deep impression made upon the mind of the Slavonic peoples by the idea of Antichrist as the type of the godless is proved by a number of sagas, songs, fairy tales, and superstitions. The saga of Gog and Magog is connected with it. This is an episode of the *Alexandreis*, in which it is told how Alexander had shut up fifteen nations under mountains near the Caucasus. These peoples will appear at the time of Antichrist and do all manner of cruel deeds. Exactly similar to this is a legend of South Russia. The legend of Antichrist and of the last judgment often appear in the Russian picture or block books (*Lubočnija Kartinki*), which constitute so large a part of Russian folk-lore. Owing to the popularity of the subject, which roused the terror of the people, many descriptions were naturally put into circulation ; among them two celebrated ones, attributed respectively to Hyppolitus and Methodius of Patara. Both are well known in early Slavonic literature, and are often repeated in later adaptations.

Besides this Apocrypha, which had so great an influence, many other Apocryphal tales were early translated into Slavonic, especially the apocryphal Acts of the Apostles, of Peter, Andrew, and

Rufinus, and those were especially preferred which were most rich in miracles, and were thus best assured of a favourable reception among the people.

Lives of the saints were also translated, especially those which were full of wonders, like that of St. Theodore Tiron, who slew a dragon in a forest and afterwards became a martyr, or like that of St. George, who made the Devil speak in a statue of Apollo and drove him out of it. Especial favourites were the hermits, like the settlers of the Thebais in Egypt, St. Anthony, St. Simon Stylites, St. Macarius, whom we have frequently mentioned, then St. Nicholas of Myra, and others whose names are legion.

In equal favour were the romantic lives which more or less resembled fairy tales without their fantastic elaboration. For example, the life of St. Alexius, the man of God, St. Eustachius, and so many others, who passed through so many marvellous adventures before they obtained the crown of happiness or martyrdom.

I have named these lives because we can prove their influence on the popular literature. The heroic deeds of the one in knightly encounters with monsters and demons, or the struggles of another with the passions, have raised a loud response in the harp-strings of popular poetry, and their deeds resound in many a folk-song, in which now one now the other is particularly emphasised.

Closer inquiry into the process of this transition
from tales into ballads and from ballads into
lyrics will lead to many an unexpected result.
Thus we can show that the name of the person
disappears gradually, and a personal song, if we
may so term it, is changed into a general *imper-
sonal* one. Thus, to give an example, there is in
the Life of St. Josaphat, which I shall have to
deal with later on, a song describing how he
flees into the desert to his teacher, and gives up
riches, happiness, and splendour. Now we can
actually show how this song in this form changed
gradually in Bulgaria, Roumania, and Russia into
a *song of the stranger*, *i.e.*, of a man who bemoans
all that he has left behind in his home. Many
more examples might be given of this kind in
popular literature showing this transition : the
subject remains, but the personal accessories disappear. I must, however, return to the Apocryphal literature.

Before I treat of the complete books, I must
consider a few fragmentary works which deal
directly with the life of Christ. There is first the
*Evangelium Infantiæ*, which is not all extant. It
occurs in the dialogues of the three saints, Basil,
John, and Chrysostom, and is nothing but a kind
of *Lucidarius*. From this book many legends
have been preserved, and have been transplanted
into Christmas carols. Among these there is the

saga, well known elsewhere, of the sacred tree under which the Holy Family rested in the flight to Egypt. The tree bends low, that the Mother of God may the more easily pluck its fruit, and when the sun rises high up in heaven, it spreads its branches out so as to shade the Holy Family. Parallel passages are easily to be found in Christmas carols, in songs, and even in iconographical descriptions of the flight to Egypt.

Passing over other fragmentary Gospels, there is, further, the above-mentioned Gospel of Nicodemus, preserved, as it seems, only in an abridged and incomplete form in the Slavonic literature, but which gave rise to the "Descent of the Holy Virgin." This is, besides, one of the oldest texts of Slavonic literature. The contents of it, taken from a copy of the twelfth century, run as follows : *—

"Once upon a time the Holy Virgin prayed to God on the Mount of Olives, and begged Him to send the Archangel Michael to show her the punishments of men. Then came the Archangel with a number of angels. And she asked him, 'How many punishments are there, and are men really punished?' And he answered, 'There are innumerable punishments;' and he ordered the Angel of the South to open hell. And she saw a multitude of men and women in great anguish.

* Tihonravov, ii. p. 23 *seq.*

The angel explained to her that these were men who had worshipped created things, as gods, sun, moon, and stars, and the Slavonic gods *Trojan, Hors, Veles,* and *Perun,* and they still hankered after evil; therefore were they punished.

"Farther on she saw a thick darkness which covered the people. At her request this cloud disappeared for a moment. The punished ones could not see her, because they had seen no light for an endless time. The angel said that these were they who had not believed in the Trinity nor in the Holy Virgin. She wept bitterly over them, and went on towards the south, where there is a burning stream. In this men were lying, some completely immersed, others only partially. These were the dishonest and the cannibals, *i.e.,* those who ruined others. At one place she saw men hanged upside down, and being gnawed by worms. These were the lovers of gold and silver. Again, she saw women hanging by their teeth, and dragons coming out of their mouths. These were they that listen at doors and then tell lies. Thence the Holy Virgin went to the North. There she found a burning cloud in which were fiery beds, on which lay men and women. They had not got up on Sunday to go to church. In another place men sat on burning stools. These had not stood up before the priests in church. Again the Holy Virgin looked and saw a mighty iron tree. On its boughs hung hooks with men

hanging by their tongues. These were those who
had caused enmity between man and man. Farther
on she sees a man being eaten by a bird with wings
and three heads. With one of these it covered his
eyes, with the other his mouth, so that he could
not pray to God for mercy. This was a man who
knew the Scriptures but did not follow them.
Then she sees the punishment of unworthy priests,
who were careless in their duties or immoral in
their lives. At last she comes to a mighty stream
of fire, which boils like the water in a kettle and
tosses like the waves of the sea. Here were Jews,
heathens, and renegade Christians, who had fallen
from the true faith, and had served the Devil.

"Then the Holy Virgin arose and went to the
throne of God and begged for mercy for the souls
in torment. She called to her aid Moses the law-
giver, Paul the apostle and spreader of the Epistles,
and John the Evangelist, but all in vain. At last
she begs Michael the Archangel and the choir of
angels to pray with her for mercy from God. Christ
therefore descends, and when the tortured souls
see Him they pray to Him for mercy. Christ
thereupon assures them, at the request of His
Mother, that their punishment shall be remitted
from Green Thursday to Pentecost."

So far goes this fanciful description in an abridged
form. Similar descriptions, and much older even
than the Gospel of Nicodemus, we meet in the old

apocalyptical literature of the East. I mention especially that of the prophet Isaiah, and the old Persian in the *Arda-Viraf-Nâmeh*. Here also a priest travels through hell and Paradise, and describes at full length the punishments and the woe of hell. It is a question of special inquiry as to how far our Apocalypse was subject to the influence of the latter, with which it shows an undoubted similarity.

Besides this, there is also, as I mentioned above, another eschatological story dealing with the previous condition of the soul from the moment of its departure from the body till it reaches heaven or hell. This Apocryphon is ascribed to the Apostle Paul, who saw it in an apocalyptical vision.

In the Slavonic literature it has been preserved in two forms, an abridged and shorter one, and an enlarged one, corresponding more closely to the Greek text, and treating not only of the departure of the soul, but also of the happiness of Paradise and the torments of hell. This latter part, however, has been rendered superfluous by the account attributed to the Holy Virgin, and thus the first part formed a separate existence, in which the departure of the soul from the body is described as follows : *—

" On every day there appear before the throne of God the angels of good men who live piously,

* St. Novakovič, Primeri Književnostii jezika staroga i srpsko-slovens-koga, Belgrad, 1877, p. 437 *seq.* ; Tihonravov, ii. 40 *seq.*

and they bring their good deeds before God, full of joy and wonderment at the patient piety of man. Opposite to these appear the angels of bad men, crying bitterly, and they ask God why they should serve such men. But God answers that they should serve them as long as they lived, for perhaps they might make them better. And the Apostle Paul begged of the angel that he might see the place of the good and the bad souls. He was first taken to hell, where he saw the wicked spirits who torture bad men ; they ruled the world and received the souls of the wicked. Then he saw bright angels, who were the angels of the good, and were always ready to receive their souls at the moment of death.

" The Apostle then looked down upon the earth, and saw it surrounded by a fiery cloud. This consisted of the sins of the world mixed with prayers. He then desired to witness the death of a just man and of an unjust man. The angel bids him look down. He saw a just man and troops of bright angels approaching him, and all the good deeds he had performed on earth. These all receive his soul, and say to it three times, ' Soul, soul, look upon the body in which thou hast lived, for on the day of judgment thou shalt rejoin it.' This goes on for three days, then comes the man's angel and kisses the soul, and encourages it, for it has done the will of God. It is then led up to heaven. On the way the soul has to pass many stations

of bad angels, who refer to its sins and attempt
to drag it down. But the angel supports it, and
the soul reaches heaven unharmed, where it is
greeted and welcomed by innumerable hosts, till
finally God places it in the fields of Paradise.
"Not so the soul of the sinner. This is taken
in charge by the evil spirits. The guardian angel
weeps and accompanies it to heaven, where God
recalls its sins and condemns it to hell."

I have merely given a short sketch of the contents
of this apocalypse. This part is spun out at length
in a similar vision which St. Macarius is said to have
had in the wilderness. This is the same Macarius
who had a vision of three dead men in the desert,
which became the foundation of the *danses macabres*,
which was so called, I suppose, after the name of the
same *Macarius*, altered to Macaire, Macabre.

The next question after the end of man was
that of the end of the world. The *Apocalypse
of St. John gave an answer to it, but this was
too general for the pious and ascetic reader of the
olden times, and thus another Apocalypse was
attributed to the *same St. John*, in which he is represented as asking questions and Christ as giving
answers about the end of all things. This book,
called "Questions and Answers of St. John on
Mount Tabor," is of the more importance as it
became a standard book of the Bogomils. It was
translated in an early period by the Kathars of

Concorenzo from Slavonic into Latin, and is preserved in a much expanded form in the Acts of
the Inquisition at Carcassone, under the name of
*Secretum Hæreticorum de Concorenzio.* There
it is expressly mentioned, *"portatum de Bulgaria
a Nazario suo episcopo, plenum erroribus."* * The
Greek original has been published by Tischendorf,
and we possess Slavonic texts of the fifteenth and
sixteenth centuries. The Latin text embraces beginning and end, and gives first a picture of the
Fall, and describes how Satan first came down to the
earth. He found it resting on two fishes, and these
on water, clouds, and fire ; and then it is told how
Satan created this world. It then speaks of baptism, and finally ends with the question of the
second coming of Christ and the overthrow of the
power of Satan. This latter part forms the chief
contents of the extant Slavonic text. Here we
have also the additional trait that a mighty book is
shown to John : " Its thickness was that of seven
mountains, and its breadth so great that no human
mind could grasp it ; and this book had seven
seals. In it was written all that is in heaven
and on earth." This commencement and the Latin
version reminds us of the *Golubinaya Kniga,*
which is closely connected with it, and its origin
must be somehow brought into relation with
this Apocalypse. After this comes the story of

* Thilo, Codex Apocryphus, i. p. 884 *seq.*

E

the second coming, all in the form of question and answer, and then the signs of the last judgment. First, Antichrist will appear; he is thus described:— "His face is dark, the hairs of his head like sharp arrows, his gaze marvellous, his right eye like the rising star of morn, his left eye like that of a lion, his mouth an ell wide, each of his teeth a span broad, his nails like sickles, his footsteps each two spans broad, and on his brow is written 'Anti-Christ.' He will rise up to heaven and descend to hell, and do all manner of evil deeds to the righteous. Then 'God will turn the heaven into iron, so that it will not rain, and the clouds will disappear and the winds cease. Then will come the Prophets Enoch and Elijah, and fight with Antichrist, but will be defeated by him. Then the angels will raise all the righteous, and all holy vessels and books, into the sky, and everything will be destroyed in the conflagration of the world. The winds will then clear it away, so that the earth will be white as snow or clean parchment, prepared for the last judgment." Then follows a powerful, though fantastic, description of the advent of Christ, when the seven seals are opened, and the dead as well as Antichrist and his followers are judged.

One of the most popular legends, of quite a different character, which plays a great part in the mediæval movement, is the " Legend of Sunday,"

more often called also " The Letter from Heaven."
Known in the East as early as the eighth century,
it soon became the common property of all Europe.
Roger of Hovedene gives this "Letter from
Heaven " in his Chronicle under the year 1201,
and says that it had been brought in this year
to England by Abbot Eustachius of Flays. The
letter was directly copied thence by Roger of
Wendover into his own Chronicle. An Anglo-
Saxon translation is said to be in existence at
Corpus Christi College in Oxford. The fact that
makes this letter so important is that it became
the leading document of the Flagellants. These
first appeared in Lombardy in the thirteenth century, and spread as far as Poland and Moravia;
they then disappear for a time, only to reappear
with renewed vigour in the fifteenth century.
Contemporary writers mention this "Letter from .
Heaven" as the writing which they were accus-
tomed to read immediately after their flagellation.
In Slavonic literature, MSS. of the fourteenth and
fifteenth centuries are extant, which are derived
from the Greek, and thus render it probable that the
Latin texts also came from the same source. Its
contents, in the best known form, run as follows :

" Once upon a time in Jerusalem [other texts say
in Rome] there fell upon the Mount of Olives a
stone from heaven, which no man could raise. The
Patriarch and the whole Synod gathered round it,

and prayed to God for three days and three nights, till the stone opened of itself and therein lay a big roll with the following words, written by God :— 'I am your God, and ye are my people. I have already written twice unto you, now I write for the third and last time. Ye must fear me. I have already sent you many signs of my wrath, but ye have not hearkened. Ye shall keep holy my Sunday, Friday, and Wednesday. Do ye not know that on a Friday I created Adam? that on a Sunday the Archangel Gabriel brought the joyful Annunciation; that on a Sunday I was baptized in the Jordan; that I rose again on a Sunday, and will judge the world in that day? On Wednesday the Jews spoke together how they might slay me; therefore shall ye on that day fast, love one another, and do good. The Pagans, though they have not our faith, still do good after their belief. But ye do it not. Therefore would I have long ago destroyed you, but that the Holy Virgin and the Apostles have prayed for you that I should put off your punishment. Fast ye, therefore, and keep Sunday, Friday, and Wednesday, and I will send you my blessing. But if you do not do this, a terrible punishment will befall you. It will rain fire and hot water, wild beasts will destroy mankind, and among these will be animals having the head of a lion, the wings of an eagle, hair instead of feathers, and horses' tails.'"

It goes on to say that a voice from heaven
announced that this message came from the invisible Father Himself, and woe unto him who did
not believe it, for upon him would come eternal
punishment. Cursed be that priest or deacon who
would not read this message in church, or who did
not copy it out and send it to far lands. 'On the
other hand, he was to be relieved of all his sins who
read it and copied it.

This is the main drift of this letter, which was
copied a thousand times, and gradually was used
as an amulet. In later versions of it, help in ex-
tremity, freedom from fear, and protection against
the attacks of the wicked spirits is promised as
a reward for carrying it. Under the title of
" Letter from Heaven " or " The Lord's Letter,"
this Sunday legend had become a favourite book
for the people in Roumania and Russia, and even
serves as an amulet.

This deep reverence for the days sanctified by
events in the life of the Saviour led in the East
of Europe to a kind of personification of those
days. Instead of the good fairies of Western tradition, we have in the fairy tales of those lands St.
Sunday, St. Wednesday, and St. Friday, and we
meet with them in popular songs, especially in songs
for Christmas and New Year. Superstitions were
connected with the proper observance of these days.
The slightest work would involve an immediate

punishment. These consequences, threatened by Scripture in the form of outbursts of Nature, were taken quite literally, and to each particular deed is appropriated its own punishment, *e.g.*, a storm for needlework, and so on. We all know the legend of the Man in the Moon, a German form of which recognises in him a man who had collected a bundle of wood on a Sunday.*

Once started on the way of attributing special sanctity to certain days beyond those of the canon, the plan was soon extended to certain Fridays on which certain important events are said to have happened. This forms the "Legends of the Twelve Fridays," which is still now-a-days a popular book. The basis of this is formed by a disputation between Eleftherie the Christian and Tarasie the Jew, on the result of which depends whether the former should become a Jew or the latter a Christian. The question put by the Jew is, Which are the twelve great Fridays? Mathia, the son of the Jew, betrays them to the Christian, and tells how they had been written down by the Apostles and hidden by the Jews. I may give here from a MS. of the fifteenth century the first three :—

"The first Friday is on the 6th March ; on this day Adam transgressed the command of God and was driven out of Paradise. The second Friday is before the Annunciation ; on this Cain killed Abel and brought death into the world. The

* Gaster, Lit. Pop., p. 371 *seq.*

third Friday is that of Christ's crucifixion; on this He sacrificed Himself for the redemption of sinners." And so it goes on. The later the text, the more details are given to each day, in order to make them more important and to encourage observance of them and fasting upon them. The most important example of all this literary influence is the *Golubinaya Kniga, i.e., Glubinaya: the Mysterious book,* with a translation of which I conclude this sketch of the apocryphal literature. It is one of the most widespread and most celebrated of Russian folk-songs, and forms the centre of all recent inquiry into Russian folk-lore. Its contents will sufficiently explain the interest which attaches to it. I have selected the variant which seems to be most complete.*

" In a land far in the East—arose a dark grey cloud.

" From the dark grey cloud—fell the Golubinaya Kniga— upon the light-giving, life-giving Cross.

" Round this Kniga—collected forty Tzars and Tzarevitch— forty kings and princes—with many dukes and boyards.

" Among them were five Tzars, the greatest Tzars—Isaj Tzar, Vasilej Tzar—Tzar Volontoman Volontomanitch—and the wise Tzar David Essevitch [son of Jesse].

" Then out spake Tzar Volontoman—' Who among us, my brothers, is skilled in reading? that he may read this Kniga Golubinaya—and tell us of the white world—out of what the white world is made—and of what the beauteous sun—and of what the moon with her soft light—and of what the crowded stars—and of what the glorious gloaming—the twilight of the eve, the twilight of the dawn?'

* Bezsonof, Kalêki Perchožie, i., Moscow, 1861, No. 81, p. 293 *seq.*

"Then stood the Tzars all silent.

"But the answer gave the wise Tzar—David Essevitch—' I, my brothers, will speak unto you—about the Golubinaya Kniga —John the Priest (Bogoslov) wrote it—the Prophet Isaiah read it—for three years he read it—and yet 'twas but three leaves.

"' I will tell you by heart what was in this writing :—the world arose—from Christ the Tzar of heaven,—The beauteous sun arose from God's bright face,—from His bosom the moon with her soft light,—from his robe the crowded stars,—the red sky of eve and dawn from the eyes of God.'

"Thereon bowed all the Tzars (and said)—' O thou wise Tzar—David Essevitch—tell us too—let us know—from what we Tzars arose—from what the princes and boyards—whence the true believers—whence the men ? '

"Answered then the wise Tzar—' We Tzars have our origin in the head of Adam—the boyards and princes from his rib— the peasants from his knees—from him too arose the race of women ;—our body is out of the moist of the earth—our bones out of stones—our blood out of the Black Sea—our thought of the clouds.'

"Bowed the Tzars and gave their thanks—and said—' But tell us—who is the greatest Tzar,—which town the mother of all towns,—which church is the mother church ?'

"He answered—' Our wise Tzar is the greatest—because he believed in the holy Christ—his hand is stretched over all— over the whole inhabited world—therefore is he mightiest.— Jerusalem is the mother of all cities—because she stands in the centre of the world—in the midst of the famous city stands the cathedral—the holy of holies of the Mother of God—and of the resurrection—in this church is the tomb of Christ—ever is incense and *ladan* burning there—hence is this the mother of the churches.'

"The Tzars thanked him—and asked—' Which are the most important—which lake,—which fish,—which bird,—and what beast is the mightiest of all ?'

"The wise Tzar answered—' The sea of ocean is the mightiest

—it surrounds the whole earth—out of the sea of ocean arose
the cathedral—of the holy St. Clement.—Lake Ilmen is the
mightiest of all—not the one in Novgorod—but that one—in
the Turkish realm—this Ilmen is near Jerusalem—and from
it rises Little Mother Jordan.—The mightiest of fishes is the
whale—for the earth rests on three whales.—The bird strefil
(ostrich) is the mightiest of birds—it lives in the midst of the
sea—and eats and drinks after prayers—two hours after midnight—the strefil shakes himself—at once dawn breaks—and
all the cocks they crow.—The mightiest of beasts is the unicorn—he lives on Mount Tabor—walks under the earth—and
cleans the brooks and wells—wherever this beast goeth—the
wells boil over—when he comes back—all beasts bow down
before him.'

"The Tzars thanked him—and asked him—'Which mount
is the most important—which stone,—which tree,—and which
herb?'

"The wise Tzar answered—'The Mount Tabor is the most
important—because in it Christ was announced—before His
apostolic disciples—to whom He showed great glory.—The most
important stone is the white *Latyr*-stone (altar-stone)—Christ
stood on it as He talked with the disciples—established the
Christian faith, and spread the Bible over the earth.—The
cypress is the greatest tree—for out of it was moulded the
wondrous cross—on which Christ was crucified.—Willow-herb
is the greatest—as the Mother of God—was going to her son—
her tears fell on the moist earth—whence sprang the willow-
herb.'

"The Tzars then bowed—and said—'Yester morn came
two hares—from far afield—one was grey, the other white—
they tore one another—till the grey one conquered the white.
—The white one went into the bright field—the grey one into
the darksome wood;—what sins will never be forgiven?'

"The wise Tzar answered—'The two hares are Justice and
Injustice—they struggle with one another—Injustice conquers
Justice—Justice goes to heaven above—to Christ Lord—In-
justice came to this world—to the people—and hid herself in

the heart—hence unjust deeds—He that insults the Holy Ghost —for his sin there is no repentance—neither in this nor in the future world.' "

In this folk-song the whole Apocryphal literature of the Old and New Testament is portrayed. The variants omitted here show other well-known traits. In all of them, however, we recognise without hesitation the dualistic and Bogomilistic origin, which is clearly expressed in the justice in heaven and the injustice on earth. We recognise in it parallels with German mythology, traces of the Physiologus in the cosmogony, and what is more, the saga of the San-Gréal in the puzzling latyr-stone, which I have translated *altar-stone.*

# IV.

*EXORCISMS AND SPELLS.*

# IV.

I HAVE already touched upon the translation of the Apocrypha of the New Testament into *amulets, i.e.*, into means for producing wonders or good health, quite apart from their legendary contents.

Here we come across an important division of general folk-lore, viz., exorcisms and spells directed against disease, regarded as an evil spirit. According to old notions, the enemy of man could be the sole author of all sorrows. In an Old Slavonic legend it is said that when God created Adam and left his body on the ground before putting the soul into it, Satanael came and put upon Adam seventy diseases. When God bade him take them away again, Satanael caused them to enter the body, and told God that unless man suffered he would never think of God. In this way man remained troubled with pains.*

In the New Testament many examples are given of men possessed who were freed by Christ, and of invalids who were healed by the Apostles. We have, too, the invulnerability of the Apostles, as in the story of St. Paul and the viper. The more the

* Pypin, *l. c.*, pp. 12-13.

view grew of this evil power of Satan, as it naturally would ˙from a dualistic standpoint, such as that of the Manichæans and other heretics, the more must the healing powers of the saints increase. They had to free man from the power of the arch-enemy.

The belief in Satan and the legends relative to the worship of.the Devil under the form of a cat, with all the orgies attributed to the heretical sects, has been further the origin of all the tales connected with witches and with sorcery. It lies outside of the limits of the present inquiry to follow out this connection, and to prove that the accusations against the latter have not been anything else than a transfer from the extirpated Cathars or Bogomils or Manichæans to the innocent victims of fanaticism and ignorance. The witches too worship Satan, acknowledge his power, sell their souls for earthly benefit and might, and become thus dreaded foes of their fellow-citizens.

The very name of *Vaulderie*, denoting witch-craft, is derived from the *Vauldois* or Waldenses, just as *Boggard*, a Northern provincial appella-tion of a foul fiend, evidently resolves itself into *Bulgard* or Bulgarian, the very common designa-tion of the *Albigenses*, whose dealing with Satan was notoriously a general belief.* They are, like their master, the cause of every disease, and the

* *Cf.* G. S. Faber, Valdenses, London, 1838, p. 339, No. 1.

exorcism is employed as well against them and
their witchcraft as against the direct work of the
evil spirit. The parallelism between the witches
and the heretics is perfect, the one being the successor of the other.

The belief in witchcraft can scarcely be traced
in Europe earlier than the fourteenth century, and
ranges in time also exactly with the appearance
and spread of the dualistic creed.

As soon as the belief was established that disease is the work of an evil spirit, its remedy took
a symbolic form. Certain ceremonies were adopted,
and a saint was called upon who in his lifetime
had fought against the *same* spirit, and had defeated him. First among these, of course, we must
take into account Christ Himself, to whom the
patient has resort, trusting that the illness once
healed by Him will be again cured. Then very
frequently the Holy Virgin was invoked, generally
as an interceder for the sufferer, and so the invoca-
tions go on to apostles and saints. Any one who
has looked through the German *Romanus-büchlein*,
the French *Enchantements* (Nisard), or the English
superstitious rhymes of Chalmers and Halliwell, or
the earlier collections in Delrio (*Disquisitio Magi-
carum*), will meet at every turn with such invoca-
tions and spells. They are equally numerous, if
not more so, in modern Greek, Slavonic and Roumanian folk-lore. Especially well known and cele-

brated is a formula of incantation against the twelve
fever-fits (*Tresêvica*). This is attributed to Popa
Jeremiah himself, the founder of Bogomilism.
They are quoted as such in the old *Indices Ex-
purgatorii.* There is no doubt, therefore, that the
spell is derived from the East, and I have elsewhere
proved its existence in that quarter as early as the
eighth century. It may have been of Manichæan
origin, and probably was translated and adapted
by Popa Jeremiah himself. The spell has been
preserved up to the present day in all the lands
of East Europe, and, with certain modifications,
also among Jews and Germans. The legend runs
as follows :—

" St. Sisinie was a brave warrior. Once upon
a time the Archangel Gabriel appeared to him in a
dream, and told him to go to his sister Melintia.
She had had five children who had all been stolen
by the Devil, and was about to give birth to a sixth.
Sisinie was to pursue the demon and obtain the
children back from him.

" His sister had made for herself a marble pillar,
and had shut herself in it. When Sisinie made
himself known to her, she opened the door. But
the demon had changed himself into a millet-
seed, and came in with him under the hoof of his
horse. He steals the child and flies away. St.
Sisinie pursues him, and as he passes a willow tree,
asks it if it has seen the demon with the child.

This deceives him, and says No, and is thereupon cursed by St. Sisinie with the curse that it shall only blossom but bear no fruit. Then he asks a briar, which likewise deceives him. This shall have its head in the earth, and all men shall become entangled in it, so that they will curse at it. At last he asks the olive tree, which tells the truth and receives a blessing for it.

"The saint accordingly casts his line into the sea, and pulls out the demon, and beats him with seventy-two fiery clubs till he shall restore the six children. He says he will give the children back when the saint shall be able to give back all the milk which he has taken from his mother's breasts. St. Sisinie does this by aid of a miracle, and the demon has to return all the six children he had stolen, and the demon promises to keep away from every house where the prayer (or formula) of St. Sisinie was to be found." *

The prayer or formula referred to here in the text has freed itself and acquired an independent existence, or, as I would prefer to assume, it existed even before the legend. This, though attributed to Sisynios, the immediate follower of Mani, as chief of the Manichæans, seems to have been derived from an earlier Oriental tale, which became the basis of all later formulæ. I give it here in the Roumanian form, which closely resembles the old

* Gaster, *l. c.*, p. 393 *seq.*

F

one. It may be observed that here, as in all the other variants, the demon is a feminine one. The following is the legend :—

"I, Sisoe, as I came down from the Mount of Olives, saw the Archangel Gabriel as he met the *Avestitza* wing of Satan, and seized her by the hair and asked her where she was going. And she answered that she was going to cheat the Holy Virgin by her tricks, steal the new-born child and drink its blood. The Archangel asked her how she could get into houses so as to steal the children ; and she answered that she changed herself into a fly or a cat, &c. But whosoever knew her twelve (19) and a half names and wrote them out, she could not touch. She told him these names and they were written down."

There is a Coptic parallel to this, more or less identical, as well as a Greek and Slavonic one. The fairy who steals children is called *Lilith*, and is further identified with Herodias and her twelve daughters, as personifications of different kinds of fever.

The vicissitudes of this belief in the Middle Ages are too well known for me to do more than refer to them. Everywhere *vilas, elves, fairies*, and similar female beings lie in wait for children. The part they play in the whirlwind of the German myths connects this belief, which might appear to be very old in Europe, with this female demon of the Oriental tales.

The characteristic point is that this female spirit is everywhere regarded as the cause of *catalepsy* or fits. Hence the invocation to St. Sisinie as driving these away. Then this invocation is used as an amulet and spell. I add the translation of one of these from the Roumanian, in which the Holy Virgin is taken as the healer. In the Russian parallel the names of the twelve daughters are taken as personifications of the disease. The Roumanian formula is against *cramp* in the night.

"There is a mighty hill—and on this hill—is a golden apple-tree.

" Under the golden apple-tree—is a golden stool.

" On the stool who sits there?

" There sits the Mother of God—with St. Maria. With the bow in her right hand—with the cup in her left.

" She looks up and sees naught—she looks down—and sees Mr. and Mrs. Disease.

" Messieurs Cramp and Mesdames Cramp—Mr. Vampyre and Mrs. Vampyre—Messieurs Wehrwolf and Mesdames Wehrwolf. They are going to N. N.—to drink his blood—and to put in him a foul heart.

" The Mother of God—when she saw them—went down to them—spoke to them and asked them—' Where go ye—Mr. and Mrs. Disease?' &c.

" ' We go to N. N. his blood to drink—his heart to change to a foul one.'

" ' No! ye shall go back—give him his blood back—restore his own heart and leave N. N. immediately.' . . .

" Cramps of the night—cramps of the midnight—cramps of the day—cramps wherever they are. From water—from the wind—go out from the brain—from the light of the face—from the hearing of the ears—from his heart—from his hands and feet—from the soles of his feet.

"Go and hide—where black cocks 'never crow—where men never go—where no beast roars.

"Hide yourself there—stop there—and never show yourself more.

"May N. N. remain—pure and glad—as he was made by God—and was fated by the Mother of God.

"The spell is mine—the cure is God's."

I will now give a few more of the Old Slavonian spells which are connected with holy persons. These are especially directed against diseases from which the saints suffered, and from which they were freed by their inborn divine power.

Thus we have the following formula, dating from 1423, against snake-bite, under the title "Prayer of St. Paul against Snakes," just as we had before a similar prayer of St. Sisinie : *—

"In the name of the Father, the Son and the Holy Ghost, I was once a persecutor, but am now a true follower; and I went from my dwelling-place to Sicily, and they set light to a trunk, and a snake came therefrom and bit my right hand and hung from it. But I had in me the power of God, and I shook it off into the burning fire and it was destroyed, and I suffered no ill from the bite. I laid myself down to sleep, then the mighty angel Michael appeared to me and said, 'Saul, Paul, stand up and receive this writing,' and I found in

* Tihonravov, *l. c.*, ii. p. 291.

it the following words :—I exorcise you sixty and a half kinds of beasts that creep on the earth in the name of God, the Creator of heaven and earth, and in the name of the immovable throne. Serpent of evil, I exorcise thee in the name of the burning river which rises under the footstool of the Saviour, and in the name of his incorporeal angels. Thou snake of the tribe of basilisks, thou four-headed snake, twelve-headed snake, variegated snake, dragon-like snake, that art on the right side of hell, whomsoever thou bitest thou shalt have no power to harm, and thou must go away (with all the twenty-four kinds). If a man has this prayer and this curse of the true holy Apostle, and a snake bites him, then it will die on the spot, and the man that is bitten shall remain unharmed, to the honour of the Father, the Son, and the Holy Ghost, now and for all time. Amen."

Here we have then another kind of prayer like the one above of St. Sisynios but attributed to St. Paul, and already in form of an amulet in 1423. Another example may be given of a " prayer against toothache, to be carried about with one : " *—

" St. Peter once sat on a stone and wept. Christ came to him and said, ' Peter, why weepest thou ? ' Peter answered, ' Lord, my teeth pain me.' The Lord thereupon ordered the worm in Peter's tooth to come out of it and never more to go in again.

* Novaković, Primeri, p. 516.

Scarcely had the worm come out when the pain ceased. Then spoke Peter, 'I pray you, O Lord, that when these words be written out, and a man carries them, he shall have no toothache.' And the Lord answered, ''Tis well, Peter; so may it be.'"

In the North of England we find the same charm against toothache, in the *same* wording :—

> "Peter was sitting on a marble stone
> And Jesus passed by.
> Peter said, 'My Lord, my God,
> How my tooth doth ache !'
> Jesus said, 'Peter, art whole !
> And whosoever keeps these words for my sake
> Shall never have the toothache !'" *

Here is a third specimen, a charm against nose-bleeding:—" Zachariah was slain in the Lord's Temple, and his blood turned into stone. Then stop, O blood, for the Lord's servant N. N. I exorcise thee, blood, that thou stoppest in the name of the Saviour, and by the fear of the priests when they perform the offices (Liturgy) at the altar." †

I might easily add other examples to these, having their origin in the same spiritual movement. There is always some mention of a holy person who is invoked. The story itself, telling how the saint was freed from his illness, becomes an amulet, and then passes into the *spoken* literature of the people. At this stage its contents are versified

---

* Halliwell, Nursery Rhymes, p. 291.
† Novakovio, *l. c.*, p. 516.

with rhyme and refrain, as a means best adapted of fixing them in the memory. This kind of process is well known throughout the world's literature, and the most ancient literary products were preserved in this way till they were written down in book form. This happened with the Vedas and with Homer, and exactly the same always happens when anything appeals to the mind of the illiterate people and they wish to preserve it, either from superstitious or æsthetic reasons.

The whole theme is worthy of more extended treatment, for it shows us in documentary form the deep influence that Christianity in its manifold forms exercised on the thought and feeling of the people. Perhaps much that is considered to date from hoary antiquity, and has become the object of a reconstructive mythology, proves, when properly investigated from a historical standpoint, to be very much younger. The influence of Christianity on the people has been sadly undervalued, because only the higher ethical characteristics were regarded, and the miraculous and legendary elements, which have the greatest attraction for the people, were almost entirely left out of account.

# V.

ROMANTIC LITERATURE.—FOURTH CRUSADE.
ALEXANDER.—TROJAN WAR.—DIGENIS.

# V.

THE Slavonic nations owe to Greek literature not only their theological literature, but also their romances and fables. Byzantium, at the gateway of the East, was not alone an intermediary for the religious views and theological literature of the Orient, but also of its profane and poetical literature. Here, if anywhere, the traces of classical antiquity remained. To this point flowed the literature that had taken its rise on Alexandrian soil, and it was sought to keep alive as much as possible the memory of the glorious past.

One can observe in Byzantium more than elsewhere preservation and care for ancient monuments, especially when these flattered the national vanity, or did not hold out against a religious or allegorical application. We accordingly find in Byzantine literature many legends taken from ancient epic cycles. The names of Alexander the Great and Achilles, the siege of Troy and other episodes of the ancient history, are recorded with pride and vanity.

Not so the legends which have their roots in the mythology of the *Hellenes* or the ancient Greeks.

These legends, as much as the romances of Tatius, Longus, Chariton, and others, with whom the history of modern romance is closely connected, these all are carefully excluded. In Byzantium the theological spirit ruled with overwhelming power. Many pages of Byzantine history are filled with the records of spiritual and dogmatical struggles, of councils of war, and extinction of heresies. This was not a soil favourable for the development of joyous life and of epic poetry. The spirit of chivalry could never rise among the knights in the frock of a monk, and amongst the warriors against the tricks of Satan.

The Greek Orient preserved, therefore, the memory of bygone days, and only the romantic tales of prominent figures of the Greek antiquity were changed, elaborated, and widely spread, if not altogether turned into- a religious legend. This state of things, however, underwent a change, as it seems, at the close of the tenth century, when we meet a peculiar offspring of the Greek epic muse in the poetical account of the heroic deeds of *Digenis Akritas*, which we shall come across later on.

No doubt the Oriental poetry, especially that of the Persians, must have been more or less known at that time in Byzantium, and the intercourse between the far East and the Greek empire became a frequent one.

The fables and apologues of India appear, are

translated and circulated, and in their footsteps came surely also a very richly developed *oral* folk-lore.

At a fixed time, and from these Oriental sources, which we can follow step by step in their wandering from nation to nation, a new form of literature arose in the Middle Ages, the *literature of novels.* These were Oriental, for the most part Indian tales, which were collected together in one framework, and were originally intended for didactic purposes. They were intended to be the mirrors in which the Eastern princes and autocrats should see themselves, and learn lessons of justice and mildness in the form of tales and talks. These tales were gradually released from their framework, and began life on their own account. They formed most of the materials for Provençal and Southern French poets of fabliaux, and having been early brought to Italy, the novel received its most artistic form at the masterly hand of Boccaccio. Their somewhat free and sportive though attractive contents answered to the freer views of modern life, and the Italian novels, together with their basis, the Oriental tales, spread throughout Europe with astonishing rapidity, giving rise everywhere to new poetic creations. English literature itself begins with Chaucer, who drew from these sources, and Shakespeare's genius has derived thence the elements of some of his immortal productions. The great reservoir into which this literature was poured, and from which it was again drawn, is the collection of tales made in the thirteenth century, and well known under the name of *Gesta Romanorum.* Into this everything flowed; pious legends, Indian parables, classical myths, and Roman history were received side by side, and allegorised in a clerical spirit.

The influence of this novel-literature on the peoples themselves was no slight one, nor less in importance. They received the new materials with avidity, assimilated them to the old, and created new forms out of the two. This was the origin of the literature known in England by the name of *Chapbooks,* as well as of a large number of fairy tales. I must, however, refrain from entering upon this wider field, attractive though it be, and must limit myself to the narrower one before us.

Greece has here too played the part of an intermediary between East and West. Everything that came from India to Europe was early translated into Greek, and with only one exception was communicated through the Greek.

By the side of these writings, which in their way from the East first found a welcome in Greece and the Balkan peninsula, we have to take into account a stream of oral tradition which also reached these shores. Nothing is now more probable than the supposition that oral folk-lore and

fairy tales came by the same route, and found
from thence their way to the West. As I mentioned above, Benfey has explained the communication of the fairy tales through the Mongolians,
who ruled for a long time in Russia. He suggests
that from them Indian, and especially Buddhist,
tales and stories reached the other peoples of
Europe. But we know very little of any such
connection, and the Mongolians came to Europe
as a destructive rather than as a cohesive element.
The case is quite the contrary with the Byzantines
and the Slavonic peoples, who, as we have seen,
were the introducers of an important religious
movement in the Middle Ages, which came to
the other nations not with the sword, but with
the Bible and the legends clustering around it.
We have, besides, to take into account another
point, which has hitherto been overlooked, but
which gives another source for communication
between the East and West of Europe. I mean
the *fourth crusade* in the twelfth century, in
which Constantinople was captured by the Franks,
and a new Frankish empire established there.
Now the connection with their original home was
kept up, and it is well known that travellers and
soldiers are the most important element in the
spread of folk-literature. How easily, then, could
these Oriental tales, especially since they had
taken firm root in Greece, be passed on to France,

where exactly at this time the literature of fabliaux arose. These fabliaux are versified novels
and stories taken from the most various sources.
Hitherto it has not always been possible to point
out their exact literary source; this can now be
explained by the fact that many had been transplanted from the new Frankish empire in Byzantium to the home in the West.

A future comparison of fairy tales in Europe
would probably show that those gathered in the
Balkan peninsula and in the neighbouring countries
are the more primitive and less elaborate, if those
tales are of real Oriental origin.

The question of the origin of fairy tales, and
especially of the European, is much too delicate and
controversial to allow me more than to mention it
here. I must pass on, and turn to the romances,
of which some found their way into Slavonic literature, and obtained a wide circulation.

Many of these Greek romances were hitherto only
known in a Russian form till later investigations
established the real fact that almost all these tales,
as well as the Church legends, had been brought to
the North from the South, where they had been
previously translated. In the first place, among
these is the romance of a hero who was in early
times surrounded by sagas and legends, and whose
knightly deeds, bold adventures, and early death
have moved all nations from India to Ireland, and

formed for all of them an object of the greatest
interest, and even become their pride, so far as they
could bring their own history in connection there-
with. Even at the present day the name of Alexander the Great lives on in undiminished splendour,
and many a legend is still being connected with
him. No story has gone through so many adaptations and ornamentations as the "Life of Alexander the Great," falsely attributed to Callisthenes. Each nation has changed it according to
its desires, and adapted it to its own views and
wishes. The legend of Alexander accordingly
affords one of the most instructive examples of the
influence of *written* on *oral literature,* and of the
reaction of the latter on written literature. In connection with the Alexander saga we can prove
the origin of many mediæval beliefs, especially
geographical and ethnical ones, which from the book
found their way among the people. We can also
see how, in its manifold wanderings among different peoples, it has adopted native elements, and
was handed on, enriched by them. An accurate
comparison of all the versions would doubtless
show us the artistic peculiarities of each people.
Among these versions are the less known Slavonic
and Roumanian versions. These connect themselves more with the Byzantine forms, which are
of later date, and expanded by many marvellous
episodes. At the same time they have a definite

G

religious colouring, peculiar to the country and the
time. For while in the West, Alexander serves as
a brilliant example of a *knight*, in the East he is
a *believer* in the Lord Sabaoth, and figures as a
champion of the true faith against the infidels.
He goes to Jerusalem, and there recognises the
true God. So, too, Alexander burns the temple of
the idols in Persia, and says, "If they were truly
gods, they would be able to show their power and
save themselves,"—that is, he speaks and acts like
a Christian saint.

Incidentally it may be remarked, that in this
story a fact of importance for Zoroastrian literature
has been preserved ; for in this fire, as all Parsees
believe, the old books of Zarathustra were destroyed.

The legend of Alexander meets us in the Slavonic versions in a double form, viz., as an independent story, and as forming part of Chronicles.
In the Slavonic translations of Malala and Hamartolos, the Alexander saga had been introduced
as early as the thirteenth century, unless we are
to assume that it already existed in the Greek
originals, from which the Slavonic texts were derived. The independent form is probably of not
much later date. The extent of the story is too
great for me to give any selections from it. I
will only refer to the most striking incidents, and
those which exercised the greatest influence on
the popular fancy.

" Alexander is, of course, the son of Nektanebus, the king of Egypt; he is educated by Aristotle and tames *Ducipal* (*i.e.*, Bucephalus). After the death of Philip he becomes king of Macedonia. He defeats the Tartars and their king *Atalmish.* He then goes to Rome, where he receives some marvellous gifts, as, for example, Solomon's mantle adorned with snakes' eyes, and three jewels which had twelve properties, and could heal all diseases. He then goes through the wilderness, and sees marvellous beings, with men's faces and snakes' bodies (Gorgons). The war with Darius is then related, and how he hemmed in the wild nations between the mountains; and then are described in full the wonders he saw in the wilderness, men with dog's heads, with one foot, others with one eye, wonderful ants that eat up men ; further, the pigmies who war with the storks. Then he reaches the 'Macarian' Isles (of the blessed), where he holds a conversation with the Rahmans and their king Ivant. From him he receives a flask with the water of life ; this is, however, all drunk up by his slaves, who are now elves that live for ever.

" He then undertakes a journey to Paradise, but cannot reach it, and returns. He comes across the sun-tree, which prophesies his early death. He is then led down to hell, and sees there sinners and their tears, among them Darius. He dies poisoned by Levkadiush. '

Almost each trait of these complicated contents recurs in popular literature. The description of the wonders of India was a favourite chapbook in the West. A part of zoological mythology is derived from this. In it all the legends about Gryphons and Arimaspians, and similar monsters known to classical antiquity, found a place and thence spread farther. The conversation with the Rahmans occurs again in popular riddles, and many superstitious practices and beliefs connect themselves with the Brahmany who dwell in the East, and for whose happiness care is taken. The well-known legend of St. Christopher Cynocephalos is also connected with this cycle of sagas. Thus the manifold influence of the Alexander saga, which is even to-day a folk-book, is sufficiently clear.* Sir John Mandeville also tells the story of the enclosure of the nations; and has many other wonderful facts which are derived from the Alexander saga. I might, indeed, have often referred in the course of these lectures to the Travels of Sir John Mandeville, had I not feared to repeat them, for it contains a number of the sagas we treat of.

After the *Alexandreïs* we may pass on to a second saga, which in ancient and mediæval times was considered real history, but was later regarded as a saga, and now-a-days, through excavations, has

* Wesselofsky, Iz istorii romana i povesti i. St. Petersburg, 1886, pp. 129–501.

been again placed in the foreground of historical events. I refer of course to the *Trojan War*. Already in ancient times Homer had been supplanted by the fictions of Dares and Dictys. These became the basis of the great work of Guido da Colonna, which, in its turn, became the armoury for all the mediæval representations in prose and poetry. Of the numerous adaptations I need refer here only to that translated and printed by Caxton, "Recuyell of the Historyes of Troye," the first printed book in English.

The lively interest taken by European peoples in the Trojan legend may be explained by their desire to bring their own history into connection with that of the Trojans, and to refer back their genealogy to as ancient a date as possible. Almost all the ruling families of the Middle Ages go back to Troy and Æneas. Thus, in Gregory of Tours, Fredegar, in the German *Kaiser-Chronik*, Jornandes, the Edda even, traces back the Danes to the Trojans. Finally, the English kings are directly connected with Troy through *Brut*.

In the South Slavonic literature we first meet with the Trojan legend in the chroniclers, but we find also that it existed separately. The latter treatment has only recently been met with in a MS. of the beginning of the sixteenth century, now at Bucharest. The treatment is quite short, and it is remarkably interesting owing to its modifications and insertion of heterogeneous elements. I may venture to give it here in an abridged form :—

"There was in the East a mighty city at the place Skamander ; it had fifty-six gates, out of which seventy standard-bearers could march abreast. The city was named *Troada*. In it was a mighty king named *Amor*. He had once a terrible dream, and was much terrified thereat : his queen bore him a burning torch which set the city on fire and burnt it up. Soon after this the queen gave birth to a girl. When she was six months old she was placed in a tower with dumb hand-maidens. There she grew up, and as she turned every morn to the sun, she learnt a language composed of all tongues. All wondered at this, and her father caused men from all quarters of the world to come to her and listen, and he wrote-down the words that each understood. Then they combined all the words together, and the king found that his dream referred to the son who was shortly about to be born. When he was born, the king caused him to be exposed on a lonely mountain. He was there brought up by a she-bear : after three years she was killed by hunters, and the child brought to the king. He recognised his (grand) son. He sets his daughter free, giving her the name *Magdona*, while he calls the boy Alexander, *i.e.*, in Greek, *the found* (*Obretenu*). Magdona paints the picture of

a man, and when any one asks for her hand, she
answers that she will only take him for her husband who resembles the picture. One day she
saw a man riding through the sea, and she said to
her father, 'That is the expected husband.' He
is brought in, and it turns out that he is the king
of the Saracens, and has travelled through the
world to find the beauty whom he has seen in a
dream. Magdona is this beauty, and they are
married. On the other hand, Alexander finds out
from the Magi where is the most beautiful woman
in the world. When he learns that she is the wife
of King Sion, he orders the Magi to let him see
her in a dream and to cause her to see him in
the same way. They fall in love with one another.
After two years he clothes himself as a merchant
and travels to her with many goods. He sees
the woman whose name is *Egyluda*, and appears
with her before the king, who is astonished at
the resemblance between this woman and his wife.
Alexander flies with her, and the injured king
assembles fourteen other kings, among them King
Tog, &c., and they sail for Troas. When Alexander
and Egyluda came to Troas, the whole city moved,
and the King *Amor* said, 'My dream is being
fulfilled.' For ten years the enemy besieged
Troas without success. The King Sion had a
councillor named *Palmida*; he made an artificial
horse in which King Sion and three heroes hid

themselves. A part of the army hid itself near
the city. In the morning the whole army made
a feint of going right away. They had put the
horse-shoes on the horse pointing backwards. At
Alexander's command the horse is brought into
the city. The heroes come out of it; the others
with *Palmida* follow, and the city is destroyed.
Alexander flies to his brother-in-law, and rouses
him against the Canaanite princes and Tog, who
had marched against him. The Sultan takes their
lands, and since that time they belong to the
Saracens. The servants of King Sion had run off
with the wives of the soldiers. A reconciliation
is effected between Alexander and Sion, but the
servants fight against their lords and destroy one
another. King Sion falls and the city of Jerusalem is destroyed. Alexander then sees what
trouble one woman can bring into the world: he
cuts off her head and throws himself into the sea." *

Here we have the influence of the legend of
Solomon and Kitovras in the abduction, not to
speak of smaller details which have so changed the
legend of Troy. The other form of this legend is
based on that of Dictys, included in the Chronicle
of Malala. The legend together with the Chronicle
was translated probably in the tenth century.
Between the two there is still existing an inter-
mediate form of the legend of Troy, preserved in

---

* Syrku, in Archiv f. Slav. Philologie, vii. pp. 81-87.

the translation of Manasses' Chronicle ; this enables us to watch the transition between the two.*

The Middle Greek epic of *Digenis* has quite the character of a romance of chivalry, in which the knight seeks for adventures, undergoes danger, and wins his lady-love after many hard tasks and contests. The Slavonic translation of this was known long before the Greek text was recovered and edited. Recent investigations have not alone proved the great age of this version, but have shown the influence it exercised on the epic songs of Russia. Many *Byline*, as these songs are termed in Russia, are derived from the "Adventures of the Invincible Devgenie." We may go a step farther, and in popular tales and in Slavonic fairy tales again recognise this romance. Its contents may shortly be put as follows :—"A Saracen or Arabic Emir loves the daughter of a pious widow of royal descent who lives in Greece. He collects an army, invades Greece, and steals the girl. She has three brothers, and her mother sends them in pursuit of the Emir, and orders them not to return without their sister, or they may lose their heads. They fly like a hawk with golden wings and reach the borders of Arabia, where they kill 3000 guards, who attacked them from three sides. By this means they reach the Emir, who allows them to decide by lot which of them shall fight with him. Thrice does the lot

* Pypin, Očerku, p. 54 *seq.*

fall on the youngest, and he fights with and conquers the Emir. The latter promises to be baptized
from love of their sister. The brothers then ask
the sister how he had treated her. She had been
covered with jewels, and her face was veiled and
had been well guarded, and she says he only saw
her once at a distance in thirty days. They all go
together to Greece, and the Emir becomes a Christian and marries her. The mother of the Emir is
vexed at this, and she sends three Saracens to bring
him back. She gives them three horses, Wind,
Thunder, and Lightning. When they ride on
Wind, they would be invisible in Greece. When
they ride on Thunder, they would be heard throughout Arabia when they came back. When they
ride on Lightning, they would be invisible to all.
They come to Greece and hide themselves. The
Emir's wife has a wonderful dream; from this the
Emir learns about the three Saracens. These are
fetched from their hiding-place and are converted
to Christianity. The three horses are given to the
three brothers-in-law."

"After some time a child is born to the Emir,
who receives the names *Devgenij* and *Akritas.*
He grows quickly and becomes a perfect hero by
his fourteenth year. He tears into pieces an elk
and a bear, and kills a monster with four heads
near a marvellous brook. He is, in short, the true
hero of the romance, the previous incidents only

serving as an introduction to his adventures, which form the chief contents of the book. We are told of his fights with Persians and Saracens, quite after the manner of knights, recalling in tone and colour in a remarkable way the *Shah-nameh* of Firdusi. Of especial interest are two episodes, because they afford us parallels to the heroic tales of the North, and have, it would seem, strongly influenced certain Russian *Byline* or epic songs ; as, for example, the songs of Dobryna and Nastasia, &c. These episodes run as follows :—

Digenis fights with Filip-papa (in Greek *Philio-pappos*), one of the greatest of heroes, and then with his daughter *Maximiana*, whom he conquers. Filip-papa thereupon says to Digenis that there is a much greater hero than he is, and that is *Stratig*, with his four sons and daughter, who is an Amazon, and had hitherto been unconquered. Digenis goes to meet her, plays on a silver harp with golden strings, and wins the maiden's love. He conquers the father and the brothers, marries the maiden, and receives rich gifts from her relations. In this Slavonic version the characters have become a little mixed ; this can be checked by the Greek original. The unconquered heroine is not the daughter of Stratig, nor does he ever fight with her, but it is *Maximiana*, who is an Amazon princess. She is the counterpart of Brunhilde in Northern mythology. Stratig's daughter, in the

Greek *Ducas*, is carried off by Digenis. He is pursued by her relatives ; he conquers them and then follows a final reconciliation, as in the Slavonic. The fame of Digenis, who is also called *Aniketos* the Invincible, lives on to the present day in Greek folk-songs. He is the type of invincible strength, and even struggles with Charon, the modern Greek god of death, till he is defeated by Death. In this form he occurs in Russian and Roumanian folk-tales about heroes who struggle with death. This story has passed into a Russian song of *Anika Voinu*, *i.e.*, the hero Anika (from the Greek *Aniketos*), and it has been pictorially represented in one of the Russian block-books (*Lubočnyja Kartinki*). I have already referred to the Apocrypha of Abraham or the "Legend of Moses," which has influenced it, as well as the whole cycle of similar tales to which it belongs. These are the Greek epic romances, which have also come into the possession of the Slavonic peoples.

# VI.

APOLOGUES AND FABLES.—BARLAAM AND
JOSAPHAT.—THE WISE AKIR AND SYN-
TIPAS.

# VI.

I PASS now to the legendary biography of Buddha, which, as early as the eighth century, had been transformed into a Christian legend. The " Life of St. Barlaam and Josaphat" was attributed to St. John of Damascus, or another St. John, and was at an early date translated into Slavonic. St. Josaphat is no other than Buddha himself; he too leaves house and home, honour and throne, to follow his teacher, Barlaam, into the desert, and to lead the life of a hermit. This determination is produced in him by the sight of human misery on four occasions, just as is told of Buddha. This self-sacrifice answers exactly to the ascetic spirit of the Middle Ages and the heretical movement, and it is no rash assumption to attribute to it a part in the spread of this religious romance through Europe. In a previous part I have referred to the deep impression this episode made on the feeling of the people, and even to the present day the song is sung in Russia and Roumania which Josaphat addresses to the solitary wood where he is about to pass his life. The spread of this tale would be likewise encouraged by the poetical parables which it contains; among them

that of the three caskets of the "Merchant of
Venice." Almost equally celebrated is that of a
man flying from a unicorn, and hiding himself in a
brook, where he clings to a tree that grows there.
He sees two mice, the one white, the other black, and
they gnaw at the root of the tree, while under him
stands a dragon with open jaws. Then the man
notices a honeycomb on the tree, and he forgets everything while he eats it. The unicorn is
death, the brook the world full of evil, the tree life
gnawed away by day and night, the dragon hell,
and man forgets all this to enjoy a few drops of
earthly pleasure.

These parables were repeated times innumerable;
every one of them has its own history, and we
often meet with them in Slavonic and Roumanian
literatures.

A second biography, though not of a saint, which
I can also trace back to the East, is the "Life of
Æsop," falsely attributed to Planudes. This is
also full of marvellous tales of cleverness and wit.
Translated from Greek into Latin, these tales likewise find a place in world-literature. I have said
that this life is falsely attributed to Planudes, and
I support this conjecture by the fact that we possess in Slavonic literature a tale only differing from
it in a few of the biographical details, and which is
older than the epoch of Planudes. This is the
"Story of the Wise Akir, and the Sultan Sina-

grip, and Anadam, the nephew of Akir." There
is almost an identical agreement of this tale, the
drift of which I will give, with many passages of
the "Æsop." It runs as follows:—

"In a land, Adar, lives a king, Sinagrip. He
has a wise counsellor named Akirie, who is very
rich, but has no children. He therefore adopts
his nephew, Anadam, and educates him in the
best manner. After a time he appoints him his
successor in his post, and retires. But Anadam
wanted to destroy him entirely, so that he may soon
inherit his wealth. He therefore accuses Akirie before the king, and says he wished to dethrone him.
Akirie is taken prisoner and condemned to death.
But a friend takes his part, and hides him from the
world. When Pharaoh heard of the death of Akirie,
he sends an ambassy to Sinagrip to request that
he would send him an architect to build a city
in the air and to answer all riddles that one could
ask him. Sinagrip regrets the death of the wise
Akirie. His friend thereupon informs him that
he is alive. He is sent to Egypt under another
name. There he makes clever answers to all
riddles. In order to build the city in the air, he
binds a chest to two eagles, places a child in the
chest, and gives it a spit with flesh on it, and tells
it to hold this up. The eagles fly with the chest
into the sky. When he is up there, the child asks
for bricks and mortar. Pharaoh owns his defeat,

H

and recognises that his visitor must be Akirie.
The latter returns home full of honours. His
nephew is given up to him for punishment. He
only reminds him every day of what he has done,
which he takes so much to heart that he dies." *

This, shortly put, is the contents of the book, and
it occurs in exactly the same form in the " Life of
Æsop," with only a change in the names. The direct
source of the story of Akirie is doubtless Greek. It
is curious that hitherto no Greek text has been found
for it, and the suggestion occurs to one that the
Greek text has passed into the " Life of Æsop."
This explains the disappearance of Akirie in Greek,
and, on the other hand, the non-existence of Æsop
in the Old Slavonic literature. The Oriental
original is preserved in the " Arabian Nights," even
the names there corresponding. Akirie is called
*Heykar,* and Sinagrip *Sinharib, i.e.,* the Biblical
*Sennacherib.* The story, however, goes farther
back, and the journey through the air and the
riddles connect it with the Solomonic cycle ; for
the Oriental fable tells of Solomon, how he flew
through the air, carried by a demon. Out of this
was later made a flying carpet, a flying chest, and
even a flying horse, as we meet with them in the
fairy tales of all parts of the world. It is also re-
ported of Buddha, of Nimrod, and of Alexander
that they flew in the air carried by eagles. The

* Gaster, Lit. Pop., p. 104 *seq.*

gnomes which Akirie gives to his nephew, put in
striking form like proverbs, have become popular
sayings in Russia and Roumania. The popularity enjoyed by Akirie in the past,
and even in the present, has prevented that of the
"Life of Æsop" from becoming popular, but not
his fables, which have been translated into Slavonic.
We need not be surprised to find that the number
and form of these fables varies greatly. Still less
need we be surprised that many of them have
become common property and occur as so-called
animal-fables, and in the form of fairy-tales.

We may connect with this series of Oriental tales
the important book of novels *Syntipas.* The
history of this book, originally Indian, and afterwards placed by its attractive contents at the head
of the novel-literature of the Middle Ages, is by
itself a striking example of how such literature
spread. Early translated into Syriac, it was translated into Greek by Andreopulos in the eleventh
century. From an Arabic translation was derived
a Hebrew one, then a Latin one, and it thence
found a home in all vernaculars. But during its
travels it grew larger and larger. Tales belonging
to quite a different source were introduced into it,
and it received a different name in each country.
The oldest and favourite one is *Syntipas,* the name
of a sage who takes the chief part in it. In other
versions it is called "The Book of the Seven Wise

Masters," because seven sages appear in it. Even
their number was increased, and so we get a "Book
of the Ten Wise Masters," and even "Of the Forty
Veziers." Its contents may be thus abridged :—

"After many years without a child, a king at last
obtains a son. As soon as he is grown, he gives
him to the care of the sage *Syntipas*, the wisest
man in his kingdom. Many years pass and the
prince is about to return home to his father. The
sage searches the stars, and finds a great danger
threatening the prince, and that there is only one
means of evading it, and that is that he should be
silent for seven days. This is done, and the king
is in great trouble over it. The stepmother of the
prince causes him to be brought to her, on the pre-
text of being able to cause him to speak. There is
then a repetition of the old episode of Joseph and
Potiphar's wife. The queen accuses him, and seeks
to have him killed. Then there appear seven sages,
and each tells a tale, the moral of which is that a
man should not be too hasty, for woman is not to
be trusted. In this way the punishment is put off
from day to day. The queen also appears each
day and tells on her side a story, intended to in-
duce the king not to listen to his counsellors. Thus
the fateful seven days pass over, and on the eighth
appear *Syntipas* and the prince, who, being able
now to speak, tells the truth." This is the framework story by which the others are connected, their

number being increased and the form altered as time goes on. This is also true of other Oriental tales, like the "Arabian Nights," *Pantchatantra*, &c. The novel-writers of the Middle Ages followed their example, as Boccaccio, Cinthio, Margaret of Navarra, and Chaucer. So far as we yet know the literature of the Southern Slavs, the book of *Syntipas*, as a book, has not been preserved in it. The Russian version of the sixteenth century was derived from a Polish one which came from the West. But a large number of the stories contained in it have been preserved in the folk-literature of the Southern Slavonic nations, especially in their jest-books.

On the other hand, we possess a translation of early date of the no less important *Pantchatantra*. The history of its travels is no less interesting than that of *Syntipas*. While the latter is more closely connected with the novel literature, the *Pantchatantra* is more closely connected with tales. The investigation of this connection was, as I have already said, a turning-point in the history of folk-lore, with which the name of Benfey will ever be connected.

Brought at an early date from India, the book was first translated into Pehlevi, in the mixed dialect of the Sassanide epoch. From this were made Syrian and Arabic versions, under the name of *Kalilag and Damnag*, or *Kalila and Dimna*.

These names are derived from those of two jackals,
*Karataka* and *Damanaka*, which play a principal
*rôle* in the framework-story. From Arabic it was
translated by Symeon Seth in 1080 into Greek,
and from this into Slavonic, perhaps in the twelfth
century. Owing to a mistake about the proper
names, Seth called Kalila *Stephanit* and Dimna
*Ihnilates*, and these names also occur in the
Slavonic translations. I cannot here of course
pursue the history of the Arabic version, which
was translated into no less than five different
languages, and thus passed into the folk-literature
of Europe. I will merely give a few examples out
of the Slavonic translation, which, like the Greek,
is shorter than the other versions. I will preface
these with the remark that the book is attributed
in Slavonic to St. John of Damascus, owing to a
mistake about the title, because Seth was said to be
also of Damascus.

*Of a Merchant.*—It is related that in a certain
city there was a merchant who wished to travel
on business, and left some iron with a man as
a pledge. When he came back, he went to the
man with whom he had left the iron, and said
to him, " Friend, give me the iron that I left
with you." He answered him, " I placed your
iron in one of my cellars, and the mice have
eaten it up. But do not trouble yourself about
that, for you have come back safe and sound.

Come to us one of these days, and we will have
a feast and rejoice over your return." The other
man agreed, and came to eat with him. After
dinner he went home with him. There he saw
the son of the man with whom he had left the
iron, seized him, carried him to his own house, and
hid him there. Coming out again, he saw the
man seeking everywhere for his son. He then
said to him, "If you are looking for your son,
(know) that I have seen an eagle carrying him
through the air." But the other turned round
and said, " Have you ever seen an eagle carrying a
man ? " But the merchant answered, " In a place
where mice eat iron, an eagle can carry a man
away." The other understood, and gave him back
his iron, on which he gave him back his son.*

Here ends the story, which recurs in innumerable
jest-books. Another story is the celebrated fable,
La Fontaine's *Perette.*

" There was once a poor man who had received
from a friend some .butter and honey, which he
hung up in a pot. One night he thought to himself and said, " I'll sell this butter and honey ;
with this I'll get ten she-goats, and these will in
five months give birth to as many kids. In five
years I shall have at least 750, and so they will go
on increasing. I shall then sell them, and buy
100 oxen, with which I will plough, and from their

* A. Viktorov, Stefanit i Ihinlat, Moscow, 1881, pp. 32-33.

produce I shall become very rich, and build a
house four storeys high and covered with gilding,
and I'll buy several slaves and marry a wife.
She shall bear me a son, who shall be called *Pan-
gel*" (*i.e.,* "in all good"), "and I'll bring him up
as I like; and if I find him disobedient, I'll punish
him with this rod." At this he seized the rod
which lay near him, and, without intending it,
struck the pot with the butter and honey and
broke it, and the butter and honey ran away.*

As in the Greek original, the Slavonic contains
in addition the chapter on the king's dreams, which
is wanting in the Arabic version, while it still exists
in the Syrian and Tibetan versions. These symbolic dreams and their interpretations exist independently, with the title "The Dreams of the
Tzar Mamer and Shahaisha." Besides these, other
Oriental tales are included in the Slavonic MSS. ;
these, it may be conjectured, also occurred in the
Greek original, and were translated from it.

.     .     .     .     .     .

Having arrived at the conclusion of this short
sketch of the Greeko-Slavonic literature, I may
take a short retrospect of the line of argument.
The first thing that meets us is the fact, established by numerous examples, that we can no
longer consider the soul-lives of the European
peoples in the Middle Ages as independent from

* Viktorov, *l.c.,* p. 67.

one another. Paths lead from one nation to another, along which passes a literature which exercises a *uniform* influence on all, the traces of which are to be found not alone in mediæval, but also in modern folk-lore. It follows, further, that the literature of the people, as we now have it, is throughout dependent on a previous *literary* period. It is from literary works that there passed into the consciousness of the nations almost all legends, sagas, fairy tales, and even amulets, spells, and other superstitious customs.

As a third result, we have seen that the common sources out of which these have been derived are mostly of Oriental origin, and are seldom known in Europe *before the tenth century.* It is by no means implied that the peoples of Europe had nothing of the sort before, or that no mythological views were prevalent in earlier times. Nature abhors a vacuum, and so does the human mind. But the earlier possessions must have been of poor and unenduring quality, and few positive traces can be shown of this early mythology. The similarity of legends and customs which used to be given as proofs for the existence of a mythology, and that the same for all nations, will henceforth be considered as proofs to the contrary. Not a little of this folk-lore can be traced back to one and the same literary source, and we have therefore explained the identity of legends and customs

amongst different nations of Europe, not by means of
any hypothetical identity of their mythology, but by
the actual identity of their literary substratum.    I
have had to confine myself to narrow limits, otherwise many other Oriental and Christian legends
might have been traced through all forms of folk-
literature in their subsequent changes ; at first saga
or legend, then chronicle, knightly adventure, and
fairy tale, then epic, and finally lyrical song.    Reminiscences of these might have been found in
superstitions, customs, and habits.    Further, their
influence on art might have been traced in iconography and sculpture, and many other branches.

The few examples I have adduced will have
proved, I hope, that the folk-literature of Western
Europe is derived for the most part from the literature of the East, and especially from the Christian
and Buddhist literatures.    We have recognised
in Greeko-Slavonic literature the chief, and often
the only factor, in the communion of East and
West.    Apocryphal and imaginative works, early
introduced into Greece, were brought thence into
the Slavonic lands, and the missionaries of dualism
thence carried to all quarters these religious tales,
which were easily taken up and assimilated by the
people.    It was also from the South-East, and probably by oral tradition, that the knights and
soldiers of the fourth crusade brought romances
of chivalry and Buddhistic fables, which must

have found their way with other works from
India through Persia and Asia Minor to Byzantium and the Balkan peninsula. The veil that
has hitherto hidden the history and importance of
Slavonic and Middle Greek literature is gradually
beginning to be raised, and we obtain a new fertile
source for the critical inquiry of our time. The
connection between Western and Greeko-Slavonic
literature has been broken and their unity dissolved, and I shall consider myself fortunate if it
is granted to me to have restored this connection,
and to have shown, even if only on a small scale,
that all these elements worked harmoniously together in religion and poetry, fable and tale, creat-
ing a new birth of the spirit in Europe, the results
of which are to be seen in the civilisation of
to-day.

# VII.

*THE SLAVONIC PEOPLES IN THE BALKAN PENINSULA.—ORIGIN OF THE SLAVONIC LITERATURE.—CYRILL AND METHOD.*

# VII.

AFTER the brief sketch of Greeko-Slavonic literature given in the preceding pages, it is absolutely
necessary that we should attempt to form some idea
of the background on which our picture was painted.
I must content myself here with the merest sketch
of the most important events which took place
in the Balkan peninsula, viz., the invasion and
settlement of the Slavonic tribes, their struggles
with the Greeks, the arrival of the Bulgarians, and
the influence exercised by them on neighbouring
peoples. We shall then come to the conversion
of the Slavs to Christianity, the two apostles of
the Slavs, Cyrill and Method, the inventors of the
Slavonic alphabet and the founders of Slavonic
literature.

Probably no country in Europe, with the exception of the neighbouring Roumania, has been the
scene of so many invasions and raids as the Balkan
peninsula. It was the first stage reached by the
Aryans as they crossed over from Asia, at first the
mysterious Pelasgians, then the Hellenes, who supplanted them, then the Thracians in the north,
with their numerous tribes and divisions. If the

Albanians, as is generally assumed, are descended from the Thracians, then these last two peoples, the Hellenes and Thracians, have kept their hold on the Balkan peninsula to the present day.

Innumerable are the names of the more recent peoples who have passed through the peninsula, from the Gauls to the Romans, Goths, Huns, Avars, Petchenegs, and Cumans. I merely mention these names and pass at once to the Slavs, who more nearly interest us. Nor will I go into the question of the original home of the Slavs. Suffice it to remark, that the Bulgarians and Servians of to-day were originally identical with the Slovenes in Pannonia, and that they wandered from there in the course of many centuries into Mœsia, which had been laid waste and depopulated by the hordes traversing it. At last, in the fifth century, they became powerful enough to undertake expeditions on their own account against the Byzantine empire. Many investigators place the Slovenes in Roumania about this time, basing their conclusions on the Slavonic place-names. Some have gone so far as to call the ancient Dacians Slavs. Critical investigation brings to light the fact that these Slavonic place-names are of comparatively recent date, and bear trace of specific sounds which belong to a late period of the Slavonic language, when this began to split up into dialects and came under Bulgarian influence.

The Slavonic population of the Balkan peninsula

displayed no power of cohesion, just as that of
Russia failed to show any in the early period. Its
organisation is that of the clan, each clan being
settled in a separate hamlet, with its *knez* at its head.
This word, which in Slavonic, and thence in Roumanian, means *leader* or *chief,* is of peculiar interest,
as it is borrowed from the Goths, among whom the
word appears as *kuni.* The English word *king* is
absolutely identical with it, coming through the
O. H. G. *cunic,* A.-S. *cuning.* It is further well
known that in consequence of the Arian movement
Bishop Ulfilas, the translator of the Bible into
Gothic, led part of his people across the Danube
and settled in Mœsia, and it is from this quarter
that the Slavs, who arrived there later, took this
name. This may serve us as an index to settle
the date of the invasion and settlement of the
Slavs in the Balkan peninsula. This must have
been consummated about 670 A.D. Even earlier than
this Byzantine chroniclers mention struggles with
the *Sklavinoi.* Thus Constantine II. led an ex-
pedition against the people of the land called
Sklavinia in 657 A.D., and conquered them.

A turning-point in the political life of the
Southern Slavs is formed by the invasion of the
Finno-Tartar nation of the Bulgarians, who came,
under the guidance of *Isperich,* in 679 A.D. from
the north through the present Dobrugea to Mœsia.
Like the German Varægians in Russia, they col-

lected their scattered clans and united them into one nation, to which they gave their name, unlike the Varægians, whose name disappeared.*

The few relics of the Bulgarian language which still remain—mostly consisting of proper names —do not permit us at present to determine exactly their ethnological character. The most recent hypothesis is that they are related to the *Tchuvashians*, whose descendants, it is probable, are the present Tartars at Kazan. The name *Bulgar* has been connected with that of the river *Volga*. They certainly belong to the great family of *Turkish* peoples who ruled in South Russia for centuries, and of whom the Chazars are the best known. They did not come, however, alone, but with them came also Finnish tribes, absorbed afterwards into one nation.†

Contemporary writers have given us a few details about their customs, which confirm· this guess. I will merely mention their burial customs. As soon as a great man died, he was laid out in a mortuary in which were also shut up his favourite wife and his slaves. They occur most frequently in South Russia, and in Roumania. As regards this point Bulgaria is still a *terra incognita*.

The number of these conquerors cannot have been inconsiderable, as it took two or more centu-

---

* *Cf.* Jireček, C. T. Geschichte der Bulgaren Prag, 1876, p. 126 *seq.*

† Miklosich, in Miscellanea di Filolologia e Linguistica Florence, 1886, pp. 1-4.

ries before the Bulgarian language died away, and
conquerors and conquered were remodelled into a
new people. This period is filled with mighty
struggles which roused the Byzantine empire, as
under Krum, Boris, Ormortag, &c. The power of
the Bulgarians spread over almost the whole of
the Balkan peninsula ; all its inhabitants were sub-
dued. By the side of Greeks and Slovenes, and
older than the latter, there was a Roman population throughout the Middle Ages known by the
name of Wallachians, and destined to play an important *rôle* in the history of Bulgaria. Besides
these there were the Albanians, and likewise scattered remnants of other peoples like the Goths and
Avars, who had settled there. Over all these the
power of the Bulgarians spread, and yet it is
generally assumed that no trace of their influence
remains. I call attention to this point, as the view
I have to bring forward contradicts all these theories.

If we observe the languages of the Balkan peninsula as they appear before us to-day, they all
betray a surprising similarity in their grammatical
formation. This is especially the case, as it is important to notice, in their inflexions, a point in
which every language shows itself, as is well
known, remarkably sensitive, and only loses them
under some striking influence of another language.
English is so prominent an example of this fact,
that I need only refer to this point.

Now Albanian, Roumanian, Neo-Greek, and Bulgarian, as well as Servian in part, offer us such identical phenomena, that the influence which has produced this change in all four languages must, under every circumstance, have been *simultaneous.* This consideration excludes any Thracian influence, which was first assumed by Thunmann and Kopitar, and is now generally accepted. According to this theory, the Roumanians, Greeks, and Bulgarians, through intermixture with the indigenous Thracian population, lost many of their grammatical inflexions. As a proof of this, it is urged that the Albanian, which represents the old Thracian, presents the same phenomena. But much has been overlooked which renders this view impossible, as I believe; for between the influence of the Dacians, who are supposed to be identical with the Thracians, on the Roumanians, and the same on the Slavs, intervene at least *several centuries.* It is not to be assumed that a language could have remained unchanged for many centuries, and should have produced *exactly the same* linguistic results on a quite different medium, in one case Slavonian and in the other Latin. For the moment I will not press the point that at the time of the Slavonic invasion only Roman colonies in Mœsia and descendants of Goths are referred to, whereas there is not the slightest reference to any Thracian population, though this must have been very numerous, to judge from the influence assumed. Of far greater importance is the difficulty offered by Albanian. To the present day no one has succeeded in definitely settling the linguistic characteristics of this language. By the side of the Thracian theory there exists also a Greek theory, which recognises in Albanian an archaic (Pelasgian) form of Greek. I need not discuss such an hypothesis farther. The point of interest is the grammatical similarity with the other tongues. The philosophy of language does not permit us to regard this as the original type after which the remaining languages have formed themselves. Phenomena such as those before us only occur as the result of a conflict, of a struggle between the two languages, in which *both* suffer losses, and become elevated into a third language having a higher unity. We must, therefore, regard these forms in Albanian as *late.* It would be otherwise inexplicable how a form should have been preserved in Albanian which in the other languages is undoubtedly of *later* formation. Finally, if we pass to Modern Greek, we find the same objection against a Thracian origin which we adduced when speaking of Bulgarian, viz., that there was never so numerous a Thracian population as could transform Greek in so essential a manner.

In addition to all these points we have to take into account the fact, which comes out irrepressibly in an analytical investigation of, for example, the Roumanian language; this is, that these changes must have taken place at a late period—at a period when the Latin language had already been transformed into the Roumanian; in particular, after the end of the change of consonants, but before the determination of the inflexions. If we assume that this transformation of Slavonic into Bulgarian, and of Greek into Modern Greek is of late date, we are necessarily obliged to assume some thoroughgoing simultaneous influence spreading over the whole Balkan peninsula between the seventh and the tenth century, and transforming all the tongues there and then in existence in *precisely the same way.*

But there is no other nation to whom we can ascribe this change but that of the Bulgarians, which made its appearance in so striking a manner about this time, establishing a kingdom which flourished for centuries. The number of the Bulgarians could not have been inconsiderable, as one can perceive if one thinks of the numerous populations whom they ruled. Besides, they managed to keep alive their language about more than two centuries, although in a continuous struggle with other peoples and languages; and though it passed over into these, yet not, as was previously thought, without leaving deep traces on them.

The next important factor was the acceptance of Christianity, which had a most extensive influence on the development of the Slavonic peoples; for by the side of their faith, and in consequence of their faith, there grew up for them a literature and progress.

In course of time the whole of Western Europe had been converted to Christianity; even the Slavic tribes in Moravia, Pannonia, and Croatia had been baptized. Threatened by Christian Byzantium in the south, Boris, Prince of the Bulgars, saw himself surrounded on all sides by Christians, and, to relieve himself from the threatening danger and to ensure his political security, he determined to proceed to Byzantium and to accept Christianity.

Accordingly, about the year 864–865, he was baptized at Constantinople, and received the name of Michael. It was only after a long hesitation between Rome and Constantinople that he decided in favour of the latter, and received thence the first Bulgarian bishop, by name Joseph. Boris-Michael withdrew in old age into a monastery, and after his death became the first Bulgarian saint. The news of the conversion of the Bulgarian ruler and of part of his people soon spread, and attracted missionaries desirous of winning over a people who had shown themselves ready to give up their old faith. I may mention specially the Paulicians or Manichæans, who came about this time into Bulgaria, and also

the Jews, who had likewise converted the Chazars
to Judaism. I draw particular attention to these
two factors, as they were of great importance in
the spiritual and literary movements of the following centuries.

The Bulgarian power reached its culmination
under Boris's successor, Tzar Samuel (893–927).
The whole peninsula was in his hands, and he
called himself *Tzar i Samoderžetz Bulgaramu
i Grekamu, i.e.*, Tzar (Cæsar) and independent
ruler of Bulgarians and Greeks. His time, and
that of his successor Peter, is likewise the golden
age of Slavonic literature, which had now found a
true home and reached its highest limit. The seed
which the apostles of the Slavonians had sown in
the West rose, strange to say, in the East. At this
point, then, I will follow out in a few words the
careers and activity of-the apostles of the Slavs.

Constandin was born in 827 A.D., of a distinguished family, probably in Thessalonica : it is not
known whether he was of Slavonic origin. He
was sent to Constantinople, and brought up at the
Imperial Court. His remarkable knowledge of
languages was peculiarly noticeable, especially of
Oriental languages. But I will not enter into the
details of his biography, contenting myself with
the chief points. He early became a monk, and
received the name of Cyril. In this character he
travelled among the Chazars, whom he is said in a

legend to have converted to Christianity. His younger brother, Methodius, who had at first held some official post, but afterwards also became a monk in the monastery at Olympus, accompanied him in his journey to the Chazars.

In the year 862 A.D. they were both dispatched by the Emperor, Michael III., to Ratislav, in Moravia, where they proceeded to develop their literary labours. They first translated the Gospel and the Liturgy into Slavonic. All difficulties which lay in their path they were enabled to overcome by aid of the Pope ; for Cyril journeyed to Rome, and the Slavic Mass was thrice repeated in the churches of Rome, with the permission of the Pope. Cyril died in the year 869 A.D. Methodius henceforth continued by himself the work which he and Cyril had begun. The Pope revived the long-disused Bishopric of Pannonia, and appointed Methodius to this See. He was also specially favoured by Prince Kocel, who resided at Blatna (nowadays L. Platten). In 885 A.D. Methodius died at Velegrad, then the capital of Bohemia. Two years ago pilgrimages to his grave, on the thousandth anniversary of his death, were performed by all the Slavonic nations.

Scarcely had Methodius closed his eyes in death when persecution on the part of the German bishops, started already in his lifetime, was renewed with greater force. The numerous disciples whom Methodius had collected around him fled to Bulgaria, and brought with them the Slavonic alphabet. Up to a very recent time the so-called Cyrillian alphabet was regarded as the genuine work of the Apostle Cyril. But many texts were found written in an entirely different character, termed *Glagolitza*, and this was studied first by Kopitar, then by Schafarik, Miklosich, and Jagic, and, mostly on philological grounds, was declared to be the true Cyrillian alphabet, the so-called Cyrillian being of later date. The chief proof of this position—and it was more and more confirmed as time went on by the discovery of new texts — was that the texts written in this character came nearest to the language in which Cyril worked, viz., the Pannonian, now termed Old Slavonic. They were, besides, the oldest relics of the language, some of them not a hundred years later. than Cyril. The most important evidence of all was that Cyrillian palimpsests were invariably written over Glagolitic texts. A Cyrillian text is, in such cases, invariably written over a Glagolitic one that had been erased, and never *vice versâ*. This proves incontestably that the Cyrillian is later than the Glagolitic. The most important Glagolitic texts are *Clozianus* (edit. Kopitar), *Codex Zographos* (Athos, ed. Jagic), and the *Codex Assemani* (at Rome), and others.

Not a few attempts have been made to explain the origin of this curious alphabet. The difficulties

are many. In the first place, the remarkable form
of the letters ; then their no less remarkable names,
which are completely unsystematic, and, when translated, become unintelligible. All kinds of sug-
gestions have been made, none of which have led
to positive results. Some have thought of the
Runes (Hanush), others of the Gothic alphabet of
Ulfilas (Schafarik), others again of the Greek Tahy-
graphs (Taylor), and, finally, resort has been had
to the idea of a peculiar and prototypal (Greeko-
Latin) Albanian alphabet (Geitler) ; but none of
these explain either the names and arrangement
of the letters, or even their form.

I may venture to suggest what I believe to be a
new solution, which seems to me to remove the
greatest difficulties, and carries with it no inherent
improbability. As I have remarked above, the
literary labours of the brothers Cyril and Methodius
began after their return from the Chazars, where
they, according to legend, held disputations with
Jews, Mohammedans, and Schismatics, *i.e.*, Manichæans. The last were, without doubt, Armenians,
as these were at that time the chief representatives
of Manichæan ideas, and sent out missionaries in
all directions.

How easily might Cyril have adopted this Armenian or a similar alphabet, when it became known
to him among the Chazars, as most suitable for his
purpose, and have adapted it to express the Slavonic

sounds? That this must have been really the case is proved by the similarity of the Glogolitza with Armenian and Georgian, if we disregard, as is only natural, a few modifications which have taken place in the former. The other so-called Cyrillian was probably compiled by Clement, one of Cyril's disciples in Bulgaria. He took the Greek uncials as a foundation, because they were then better known, and took the characters still wanting, from the Glogolitic. Clement was later Bishop of Velica, and died 916 A.D. This is the origin of this alphabet, which drove the other from the field and usurped its name; and in this manner was the foundation laid for a Slavonic literature, with which we have now to deal. Further details are to be found in the Appendix B.

The chief representatives of this literature are the so-called *Seven Saints,* viz., Cyril and Methodius themselves, and their five immediate disciples, Clement, Gorazd, Angelar, Naum, and Sava, to whom for the most part the ecclesiastical literature owes its Slavonic form. They translated the Bible, the Liturgy, " Legends of the Saints," *Synaxaria*, as they were called ; homilies, among which the *Zlatostruj*, or "Golden Stream," deserves to be mentioned, as it was attributed to Tzar Samuel, and contains a collection of more than 100 (? 105) homilies of St. Chrysostom (Slav. *Zlatoust*). Under his auspices the Byzantine chronicles of Malalas and Gregorios

Hamartolos (Slav. *Greshnyj*) were translated, and the great Slavonic encyclopædia arose termed *Izbornik*, or " Collection of all the Important Knowledge of the Time." In imitation of the Hexaëmeron of Basil, Joanes, the Exarch, compiled a similar compilation of theological, philosophical, and scientific views on cosmogony, connecting them with the first chapter of Genesis. The book is known under the name of *Shestodnev*, *i.e.*, " Hexaëmeron on the Six Days," &c.

The impulse once given, continued through the centuries, even through the two centuries during which Bulgaria had ceased to exist, and was entirely joined to Byzantium. It continued later under the Asenides, who again made Bulgaria independent, till it fell under the power of the Turks. Tzar Samuel had often beaten the Greeks, and came near taking Constantinople ; but after his death a political decline succeeded, though the progress of thought, on the other hand, went on increasing. Under the influence of Tzar Peter (927–968 A.D.) a rich diversity of spiritual life was shown. The state was often disturbed by the Greeks, and in 971 East Bulgaria was conquered by Emperor John Zimiski. Basil II. frequently beat Tzar Samuel, grandson of Symeon, and likewise his successor, John Vladislav, who met his death in the battle of Durazzo in 1018. In the same year Bulgaria became a Byzantine province, to rebel again, and fall afterwards into the hands of the Turks until the liberating war of 1878.

The Slavonic literature became meanwhile the literature of the orthodox peoples of the South-West of Europe, and especially of the Slavonic nations. Naturally in the MSS. peculiarities of the special languages have crept in, which enable us to determine the home of each at a glance. I will only mention one of these peculiarities, though that is a specially important one. The nasal vowels ą, ę, are replaced by one or other of the remaining vowels when the MS. is not written in Bulgaria.

During recent centuries the chief place of refuge for this literature, as well as its chief place of cultivation, have been the monasteries on Mount Athos. To the present day many a precious MS. is preserved there, and from there most of the best MSS. to be found in Russia derive their origin. Thus the celebrated "Zographos Gospel," now in Moscow, once belonged to the Zographos Monastery on Mount Athos. The connection with Roumania and Russia has never ceased. Many of the most important monasteries are foundations of the Roumanian princes. The important position that Mount Athos holds for Greek literature is well known to all concerned with the subject, nor can it be said that the whole matter has been as yet thoroughly investigated. Still less can we say that we have a complete control over the whole of old Bulgarian literature. Slavonic MSS. are to be found scattered throughout all the libraries of Europe, and in many monasteries of Bulgaria itself, of Roumania, and of Russia, which have not yet been explored. But what we have in hand is sufficient to enable us to settle its extent, and determine its characteristics with some amount of precision.

# APPENDIX.

# APPENDIX A.

In close connection with the history of the Bible proper, of its translation, and of the influence it exercised, especially during the Middle Ages, is the history of the so-called *Bible Historiale,* viz., the historical part of the Bible, enriched and embellished by legendary and exegetical means, to serve at the same time homiletical and edifying purposes.

There is, however, notwithstanding its great importance, no special study which, as far as I know, endeavours to fill the gap of our knowledge in this respect, to trace the development of the *Bible Historiale* through the literatures of Europe, and to discover its probable origin. The following pages claim to be no more than an attempt to gather scattered elements and to bring this literary problem under a new light, furnished by the Oriental, and especially by the Slavonic literature with which we are dealing. There is no need to add that it is only a brief sketch, in consideration of the literature it embraces, the wide space it covers, and the results to which it leads.

Under the name of *Bible Historiale* is generally
understood the Latin compilation of *Pierre le
Mangeur*, or Petrus Comestor, vice-chancellor of
the University of Paris in the thirteenth century,
termed by himself *Historia Scholastica.* Composed
about 1175, it is the first compilation embracing
the entire contents of the Old and New Testament.
At short intervals there are also introduced special
chapters referring to the history of the world.
The author excluded from his work the dogmatical
and prophetical portions of the Bible, and the rest
is not rendered in a literal translation, but in a mere
paraphrase of the text. Sometimes this is shortened,
very often explanatory glosses of an exegetic or
polemical character are added. Not seldom the
author inserts legendary traits or entire legends
drawn from non-canonical sources. Almost every
episode is treated and commented in an allegorical
or spiritual way, and the author has often the opportunity of showing his profound learning, and his
deep acquaintance with the philosophical and scho-
lastical speculations of the time.

By the success this compilation shortly afterwards acquired it seems that it perfectly suited
the taste of the time. Not long after its appearance the book was translated into the vernacular
French, and it served as a basis and model for
many similar productions both in prose and verse
in various countries.

One question, however, has not even yet been satisfactorily settled, namely, from what sources did Comestor draw his legendary stories, and how far is he indebted to some other similar compilation?

This question is the more difficult to answer, as hitherto under the heading of *Bible Historiale* many books have been classed which bear some resemblance to each other. A closer inquiry proves, however, that there existed at least *two different Bible-histories*, one of which is the older and genuinely popular, while the second is the *Historia Scholastica*, with all its variations and translations.

A true light on this very interesting branch of universal literature is thrown on it by the older version, whose existence I am now endeavouring to prove, and which I am now going to examine independently of the other.

Before entering into this research, it is desirable to mention another work, the *Speculum* of Vincentius of Beauvais, that unparalleled encyclopædia, which comprised in one book all the different facts and ideas then current in the Christian world. In the fourth division of this *Miroir*, Vincentius passes in review and relates the history of man from Adam down to the resurrection and end of the world. Here are also inserted a number of legends and apocryphal narratives similar to the previous, and a century-older *Historia Scholastica*. This too served as a source for the following period.

The question as to the origin whence these are derived is also unsettled.

If we now compare the vernacular translations of the Bible as they have been preserved up to the present time, and if we include in this our inquiry not only the prosaic and literal, but also the versified and amplified translations extant in France and Germany, not to speak for the moment of the Italian, Slavonic, and other versions, and if we add to these the "Mysteries" based upon the versified Bible, we are inevitably compelled to affirm for a distinct part of them an undoubted independence from the *Historia Scholastica* as well as from the *Speculum.* And we must further acknowledge that they represent a different version, richer in legends and tales, less acquainted or blended with world-history and sophistical speculations, and distinctly at variance in the allegorical and spiritual explanations to those put forth in the above-mentioned works. In order to explain this hitherto unnoticed fact, we must go a step farther, and ask when and under what circumstances was the Bible itself translated into the vernacular?

There is no doubt that, curious as it may seem, with the exception of the Gothic translation by Ufilas, the Slavonic translation is the oldest extant in Europe. Above we have already traced a rough sketch of the literary activity of the two Slavonic apostles, Cyril and Method, and laid stress upon the importance which their translation had for the development of the Slavonic literature, which clusters round it as its natural centre.

Almost contemporaneously with this translation, that is, as early as the ninth century, and as a consequence of it, there appears in the Slavonic language also a *Bible Historiale*, with all its peculiar characteristics, widely circulated, and of enormous influence upon the Church and profane literature.

The Apocrypha of the Old Testament mentioned and referred to in the course of these Lectures were mostly taken from this *Bible Historiale*, in which the Biblical history is interwoven with legends.

This Slavonic Bible has a peculiar value, because it is at least *two centuries* older than the corresponding work in the Western literature, and especially than the *Historia Scholastica*, and also because it is richer in tales and legends, which on close inquiry prove to be of a more primitive and original form.

The age of this Slavonic version can be fairly well traced, as we find reference to it in the earliest Russian chronicle of Nestor. We further find entire parts of the *Palœa* embedded in the Russian *Hronographi*, just as we find traces of Biblical legends in the analogous works in the German literature, which are world-histories, beginning with

the creation of the world, and containing the whole
Biblical history, after which in these *Hronographi*
follows the Byzantine, and with this, lastly, is connected the Russian or Slavonic history.

The Byzantine literature, with the chronicles of
Malalas, Hamartolos, Syncellus, and others, and
latter on Dorotheus of Monembasia, offered the material and the example for similar Slavonic works.
They were, and this at an early period, translated ;
and the chronicle of Georgius Hamartolos (Slavonic
*Greshnyi*) in especial forms the basis of the *Hronographi*. What is now an essential point is that the
Biblical history therein contained is not drawn from
the Holy Writ directly, but from the embellished
Bible, the *Palæa*.

The references in these *Hronographi* help us
also to establish the fact that from the two *forms*
in which the *Palæa*-now-a-days exists as a shorter
one, and a more developed, the latter is the older
form, while the shorter represents only an epitome
of it. In the *Hronographi* the longer version is
generally quoted, proving thus its greater antiquity.
The difference between the two versions is by no
means essential. The text is nearly always the
same ; they vary only in the number and extent of
the legends inserted in the text. We shall meet
later on with a similar fact in the German versified *Bible Historiale*, of which there are also two
forms, a shorter and a longer, filled with legends.

So also in the Romance literatures. The Slavonic *Palæa* being all but absolutely unknown, I
will endeavour to give here a brief sketch of its
contents, in order to enable us to .elucidate the
relation in which it stands to the literature with
which we are dealing. I hope, however, to have an
early opportunity of publishing an exact translation
of the legends and apocryphal tales contained therein, with the necessary commentary.

The *Palæa*, as has been said, is an embellished
Bible ; but it would be a mistake to consider it as
a work of only an exegetical character, intending
to explain the words of the text by legendary in-
terpretation. Besides this, it has also a definite
tendency ; it is apologetic and polemic, as well as
exegetic and homiletic.

The fundamental idea developed in the *Palæa* is
that there is no event mentioned in the New Testament which has not been adumbrated and typified
in the Old Testament. The New is only the fulfilment of the prophecies and prototypes of the Old ;
hence the truth of the former, and hence, on this
theory, also the unavoidable acceptance of the New
Testament by the followers of the Old Testament.

This is the polemic argument used in the *Palæa*
against Jews, and in a less prominent way against
Mohammedans, who are often addressed directly.
We find expressions like the following scattered all
over the book, as, for example : '' Listen, O Jew ! . . .

I ask thee, O Jew! . . . O ye sinful Jews! and ye unclean Besserman (Slavonic *Musulman*). . . . Behold the wonder and thank the Lord. . . . Open your ears . . . and lift up your eyes," and so forth.

This direct attack, and the typical parallelism between the hope of the Old and the fulfilment in the New Testament is a characteristic feature of the greatest value, which I point out here, as I shall have the opportunity later on to refer to it frequently.

The *Palæa* begins, as is natural, with the description of the six days of the creation, and lingers especially at the episode of the creation of the angels, being intimately connected with the fall of Satan. According to the *Palæa*, ten hosts of angels were created at the first day. The leader of the fourth group was Satanael, who rebelled against the authority of the Lord, and was therefore cast from heaven down into the depths of hell, together with all his mutinous followers.

This hierarchy of angels is one of the most important events of creation, and the *Palæa* accordingly deals with it at some length. We have therein the accurate and minute description of the angels' rank and dignities, also which elements of nature are ruled by special angels. So there are enumerated the angels of snow, rain, hail, &c., as they are to be found in the heavenly hierarchy of Dionysius Areopagita and its sources.

Abounding with particular incidents, and very amply elaborated, is the description of the magnified works created during each day, just as is the case in the so-called *Hexaëmera*, and in the commentaries on Genesis of the oldest fathers of the Church. Among other tales, they are full of legends of animals drawn from the *Physiologus*, and other similar productions.

A large space is further devoted to the creation of men, and the entire drama the centre of which is Adam. It deals with the life in Paradise, the tree of knowledge, the creation of Eve, the various experiences Adam and Eve go through till their ejection from Paradise; and the legendary story goes on till their death; telling us, at the same time, of the travelling of Seth to the gates of Paradise, and including, therefore, the famous Legend of the Cross.

This part may be considered as the real centre of this *Biblical History*, as we have very often to refer back to it, and as all the following events are only natural consequences of the first sin, and point to the last catastrophe—the crucifixion and redemption already foreshadowed at the commencement.

We have already given (pp. 36–38) the contents of this legend. Suffice it now to add, that in the Slavonic text the oldest and most complete form of it has been preserved, which, as we shall see, is a consistent and constituent part of all the *Bible Historiales.* But whilst it is stunted in the West, losing many primitive elements, the Slavonic form by its greater completeness helps to explain it in a more satisfactory way.—The non-consideration of the latter prejudiced the otherwise valuable study of Mr. W. Meyer, as has been proved by Wessel-ofsky. The seeming incoherence and contradiction in the statement of the Legend of the Cross by Liutwin and Calderon, for instance, is made clear and comprehensible through the comparison with the Slavonic versions.

Following the account given by the Bible, we are told of the murder of Abel by means of a stone, the death of Cain, shot by Lamech, who is blind, and led by a child. We learn also all the other legends relative to the Biblical personages, and all the apocryphal stories connected with them. So also the wills of the twelve sons of Jacob, the life and adventures of Joseph, the prototype of Christ in every detail, his being sold, the temptation, &c. The life of Moses is also adorned with legends, out of which I select the episode relating to his youth. The daughter of Pharaoh brought home the child Moses to her father, who took him kindly to caress him, when Moses suddenly seized the crown, tore it from Pharaoh's head, and threw it down. The crown had an image of an idol as ornament. Pharaoh seeing this, remembered an old prophecy warning him against a son of his slaves, who would at a time depose him from his throne. He therefore considered the deed of Moses as an ill-boding omen, and ordered him to be killed. But a councillor said, "It is not right to kill a child; but let us put him to a test. Two plates shall be brought in, one filled with precious stones, the other with fiery coals, and we will place them before the child. If he stretches out his hand for the precious stones, then the child is intelligent, knows what he does, and must die; but if he touches the coals, we will desist from killing him." The two plates were brought, and Moses grasped some of the coals, put them in his mouth, and burned his tongue. He was saved, but he remained a stammerer for his life.*

We now quickly pass over the rest, as the description of the ten plagues, the *Pascha* and its identity with the self-sacrifice of Christ, the manna and its wonderful properties, the death of Moses, and the very short sketch of the Judges till the advent of David. Some texts stop at the history of Saul; others extend the narrative as far as Solomon, including all the remarkable legends of which he is the centre.

These are the meagre outlines of the Slavonic *Palœa*, two-thirds of which at least deal with the contents of Genesis and Exodus, while the later

* Gaster, Lit. Pop., pp. 318–320.

portion is added only to form the link between
Moses and Solomon, who occupies the rest of the
book.    Therefore the *Palæa* is often and rightly
called the enlarged or interpreted Genesis.

The first question which now arises, and which
I will proceed to answer, is, what is the origin of
the *Palæa*, and which the sources whence it has
drawn its materials ?    Is this book to be considered
as a genuine production of a Slavonic author, who
out of many books compiled this Bible with histories, or is the Slavonic literature indebted for it
to another, whence it was only translated ?

The name *Palæa* itself leaves no doubt that it is
of foreign, specially Greek production, just as the
other contemporaneous Slavonic literature is derived from the Greek.    The *name Palæa* is the
Greek Παλλαια διαθηκη, viz., the Old Testament,
the last word having been dropped in the course of
time.

The relationship in which the Slavonic translation stands to its Greek original is a matter somewhat difficult to decide, as no Greek text has yet
been published, and there is, indeed, only *one* copy
supposed to be in existence—a MS. in the library
of Vienna.

The texts of the *Palæa*, in spite of their general
unity, vary as to the extent of their contents, and
we find in other contemporaries of the Slavonic
literature and in the *Hronographi* legends which

no doubt formed part of the *Palæa*, and which are now missing entirely, or are found only in a fragmentary form. Some of the legends, as, for instance, that of the Cross, are further due to a remodelling by the Bulgarian heretical sects.

All these and similar considerations lead us to the conclusion that, *based* upon a Greek original, the *Palæa*, as a popular book, and a book of pronounced tendency, underwent in its Slavonic form a change during the centuries, which, however, did not alter it essentially. It became in part shortened, partly amplified by materials drawn from many sources, and developed according to special views and purposes, but all are of the same origin, namely, Byzantine, and *ultimately Oriental.*

The whole theological literature of Byzantium points clearly to the East as its cradle, and there we must look also for the origin of the *Bible Historiale.* Not a few of the allegorical interpretations meet us in the early literature of the fathers of the Church, especially such as Ephraem Syrus in his Homilies, and others. The East is also the acknowledged homestead of the Apocrypha—in one word, all the constituent elements of this literature are Oriental.

The works of Josephus, the most widely spread book in ancient times as well as in the Middle

Ages, contain many legends which passed later on
into the ecclesiastical literature, as nearly all the
writers of the Occident made large use of its
contents.

Not in these incidental references nor in these
scattered legends do we see, however, the immediate original of the *Bible Historiale*, but in entirely
similar books existent in the Jewish literature.
The connection between these later and the *Bible
Historiale* has been totally overlooked, because the
link was missing which united them with the
Western literature.

I see the most ancient instance of an enlarged
history of the principal events of the Bible in the
book called the *Book of the Jubilees*, or rather
the *Book of Adam*, which dates from at least as
early a period as one century before Christ.

This book contains the Biblical history from the
creation till the institution of the *Pascha* (Passover),
clothed in the form of a revelation made to Moses
during his stay on Mount Sinai. Here we meet for
the first time compiled in the form of a *book* nearly
all the minor legends of the *Palœa*. We are at
the beginning of the poetical and legendary activity,
which much later, and through various influences,
into which I need not now enter, developed itself
and produced the greater legends.

So we find here those relating to Cain and Lamech,
to Noah, Abraham, and his children, &c. Here, also,

we find the minute description of the creation of the
angels, and of the elements over which they preside ;
further, of the number of works accomplished in
the six days of the creation, and so on.
A characteristic feature of this book is that it
gives the names of the women of the Biblical nar-
rations.  From this treatise they enter into all the
other compilations of later times, and especially
into the *Bible Historiale*, and into the so-called
*Prophecies of Pseudo-Methodius.*
The whole matter is chronologically arranged,
and the time is equally divided into jubilees, each
of forty-nine years, hence the name of the book.
But the book is more renowned under the name of
*Leptogenesis*, that is, *Parva Genesis*—the smaller
Genesis.  No doubt the meaning thereof is *smaller*
in authority, as its size is greater than that of
the real Genesis.  It has been also termed the
*Book of Adam,* as the part he plays is the most
prominent.*
The legendary matter included in the " Book of
the Jubilees " can be shown, then, in a Palestinian
Commentary of the Pentateuch extant in two texts,
one complete and the other fragmentary.  Being

* By the way I may here mention that many other books of the same
legendary character exist in the Jewish literature, from which one is called
the *greater*, the other the *smaller*, the cause of this not being very clear.
So we have also a *Magna Genesis* (*Bereshith Rabba*), perhaps in opposition
to the above *Parva Genesis;* so, further, *Seder Olam Rabba* and *Seder
Olam Zutta; Eliah Rabba* and *Eliah Zutta; Pesikta Rabba* and *Pesikta
Zuttarta,* &c.

L

connected with the Hebrew text, this commentary
has a loose form, and not the compact arrangement
of an independent book. Its value lies in the fact
that by means of it we can pursue step by step the
growth of the legend, this commentary not being
at any rate later than the fifth century.

To the seventh century, again, is ascribed another
work, this time again a *book*, which has never been
considered in this connection—I mean the *Pirke de
R. Eliezer*, or the book called the *Chapters of R.
Eliezer*, which bears this title because it is divided
into fifty-four chapters, and the authorship is falsely
ascribed to R. Eliezer, who lived in the first century (A.C.)

But if we look nearer, we see that it is unfortunately a fragment of a larger book purporting to
be a kind of legendary development of the Pentateuch (or rather only of Genesis and Exodus),
similar to the "Book of the Jubilees," with which
it has in common calendarial calculations, and the
division of the matter in accordance with a special
view.

Out of these fifty-four chapters not less than
*forty* treat of the events contained in the book of
Genesis; namely, *nine* are devoted to the description of the creation, *ten* to Adam, *two* to his descendants till Noah, and so forth. The order of the
last chapters has been transposed, the book is suddenly interrupted, and remains without a real end.

The contents are nearly all of a legendary character, akin to that of the afore-mentioned book.

A striking resemblance to the Slavonic *Palæa* is further afforded by the last book of Jewish origin which I have occasion to mention—the *Sepher Hayashar*. The major portion of this book deals with Genesis and Exodus, the other three books of Moses, together with Joshua and the Judges, being dealt with in two to three pages out of nearly 150.

Many of the principal legends of the *Palæa* have here, I may say, their immediate source. Parts correspond word for word with each other, as, for example, the legend of Lamech, the above-quoted legend of Moses, of his wonderful rod, originating from Paradise, which becomes afterwards in Christian transformation the tree of the cross, and others we shall meet with in the course of this investigation.

Out of this *Sepher Hayashar*, together with the *Book of the Jubilees*, arose the Greek *Bible Historiale*, the original for the *Palæa*. That explains also the curious disappearance at a certain period from the Byzantine literature of the " Book of the Jubilees," which till that time was very well known, and quoted by nearly every Byzantine chronicler. As has been shown by Fabricius, and now by Rönsch, the " Book of the Jubilees " was known to the fathers of the Church as early as the fourth century; and down to the sixth century they, as well as the Byzantine writers, cite large passages from it; while from that time no trace of that book is left. *It had been absorbed by the Bible Historiale.*

That the *Sepher Hayashar*, or a very similar book, contributed to the formation of that work, there cannot be any doubt, seeing the literal agreement between the two books on one side, and, on the other, that there is no other source known for many legends of the *Palæa* and of the Western *Bible Historiale* than the *Sepher Hayashar.*

In order to become the *Palæa*, this compilation had to be adjusted to the Christian and ecclesiastical point of view. The whole matter had to be recast in a new mould, symbolical and allegorical explanations had to be added, and the work from a book of amusement changed into a book of polemical tendency.

Amongst other new elements, we can easily detect some derived from the literary activity of the Bogomils, who, like all heretical sects, eagerly adopted old legends in order to turn them, by slight changes and interpolations, into means of diffusion of their teachings. Nothing pleases the people more than allegories and parables. Therefore the *Palæa* very soon became a popular book, and exercised the deepest influence upon popular fancy and its outcome, popular literature.

To this heretical influence is due the introduction

of *Satanael,* the chief character of this dualistic heresy, and the *rôle* played by him as the patron of the earth; and especially the Legend of the Cross, which, as we know (p. 35), is directly attributed to Popa Jeremiah, the founder of Bogomilism, who is expressly mentioned as its author. Many incidents in its contents confirm the heretical origin of this legend in its present form.

This is a point upon which I lay the greatest stress, as the Legend of the Cross forms an essential part in all the different versions of the *Bible Historiale.* There is not one in the group we are studying from which this legend is missing, while the Comestor group is denuded of it.

It is one of the numerous links uniting the Eastern with the Western *Bible Historiale* to which we now pass.

In the West, France was the cradle of the study of the Bible and of its translation into the vernacular. As will be seen hereafter, traces of this translation can be followed out as early as the tenth century or the beginning of the eleventh. The oldest translations seem to be lost, and also the translations of a *Bible Historiale.* They were no doubt supplanted by the translations of Comestor's *Historia Scholastica.* But we can reconstruct the contents of that old *Bible Historiale* by many means. First of all, through the versified Bibles, some of them dating from the twelfth century (*c.* 1140) ; then through the *Mystères du Viel Testament*, based upon such a *Bible Historiale*. Besides this we have some modern copies, all of them representing an amplified text, corresponding to the amplified text of the *Palæa*. There is, finally, also an abridged form preserved in the Catalan, Bearnais, and Provençal dialect, discovered only in the last ten to fifteen years, and known to students under the most inappropriate name of *Romanische Weltchronik*. This is also nothing else than the *Bible Historiale* in a form resembling that of the ' short text of the *Palæa*.

I will now try to summarise briefly the contents of each of these works, as far as their particulars bear resemblance to those of the *Palæa* or *Sepher Hayashar*, and are independent of Comestor, thus proving their identity of origin with the former.

We start with the versified Bibles, following closely the meagre extracts given by Bonnard,* who, however, pursued another purpose in his *précis*, and is anything but satisfactory as regards his account of the contents of the texts he dealt with. A comparison with the texts themselves will furnish, I am sure, more incidents confirming the views now expounded, and perhaps some other investigator may be induced to follow out more closely what I only briefly indicate here.

* Bonnard, Traductions de la Bible en Français . . . au Moyen Age, Paris, 1884.

The first to be mentioned is *Herman de Valenciennes* (*c.* 1140), whose versified Bible extends to the history of Solomon. He cannot be thought dependent from Comestor, as he is much older than the latter, who lived *cir.* 1175. The history of the Bible is adorned by legends, amongst them the legend of Moses, different from the version of Comestor, and corresponding to that quoted above from the *Palœa*. Two plates are brought to the child, one with precious stones and the other filled with coals, and not only *one*, as is said by Comestor.[*] The *two plates* we find also in all other versified Bibles and in the *Romance Chronicle*.

Peculiar to these Bibles is the division of the world into *seven* periods, after which the end of the world shall come. At the end of some periods Herman sums up the principal events, interrupting in an abrupt way the course of the narration. Exactly the same is the case in the *Romance Chronicle*. Bonnard says (p. 26): "Par deux fois Herman fait des principaux évenements de la Bible une rapide recapitulation qui ne se lie à rien et qui coupe brusquement le récit."

This division of the history is a faint echo of the old divisions in the Oriental prototypes of the *Bible Historiale*, and the number *seven* is chosen in accordance with the seven days of the creation, alluded to already by Barnabas (cap. xii. v. 4):

[*] Bonnard, p. 16.

"Consider, my children, what that signifies, He
finished them in six days. The meaning of it is
this—that in six thousand years the Lord God will
bring all things to an end." We find it further
said by Augustinus *—and what is more important
in this connection, in the apocryphal book of the
Bogomils, attributed to St. Johannes (mentioned
above, p. 64), where it is also expressly stated—
that the power of Satan will last for seven days,
that is, seven periods.† Other ecclesiastical writers,
such as Bede, St. Isidorus, &c., adopted the same
division, current in the Middle Ages.

I mention this at some length, because, as we
shall see, it served as a proof for the supposed dependence of the *Romance Chronicle* upon Isidorus.

The legend of the Cross originating from Para-.
dise is also contained in the versified Bible, and
other particulars of minor importance.

Decidedly independent of Comestor is also the
next author, *Geffroi de Paris*. He is identical
with Herman " pour les légendes introduites dans
le texte sacré." ‡

*Macé de la Charité*, author of another versified Bible, borrowed his numerous glosses also from
another source than Comestor. Bonnard says explicitly (pp. 72, 73): "It is certain that the abundant
glosses used by Macé to adorn his narrative are not
derived from P. Comestor's *Historia Scholastica*."

* End of *De Civitate Dei*.    † *Thilo*, i. p. 890.    ‡ Bonnard, p. 43.

The foreign source can be much more clearly
proved for *Evrat's* versified Genesis. (He lived
*c.* 1198.) He cites Josephus, Bede, and Hieronymus, but surely only at secondhand. Comestor is
never mentioned, and what he quotes from the
*maître*—this is the title for Comestor in writings
of later period—is not to be found in the *Historia
Scholastica.**

On the contrary, from the brief extracts given by
Bonnard, we can recognise the identity with the *Bible
Historiale,* and the author divides the history also
into periods. We find the death of Cain caused by
Lamech. Continual reference is made to parallel
passages in the history of the New Testament, with
the same allegorical and symbolical explanations;
so in the lives of Jacob and Rachel; so is Joseph
sold for *thirty deniers,* although the Bible clearly
speaks of only *twenty* pieces of silver. This change,
made with the purpose of finding a parallelism
between Joseph and Christ, occurs already in chapter ii. of the apocryphal Testament of *Gad,* the
son of Jacob.† So also in the Roumanian "*Hronograf*," cap. xi. The comparison between Joseph and
Christ is a favourite topic of the old writers of
homilies, such as Ephraem Syrus and others.

Treating the blessing of Jacob, when Evrat comes
to Dan, where it is said, "Dan shall be a serpent

* Bonnard, p. 111.

† Fabricius, Vet. Test., i. p. 677 ; *cf.* ii. p. 79. The Slavonic translation, Tihonravov, i. p. 207.

in the way, an adder in the path," he gives at full
length the legend of *Antichrist.*

The explanation of Dan's blessing as pointing to
Antichrist is likewise given in the *Palœa,* and in
more ancient sources, such as Hippolytus and St.
Theodoret of Cyprus (457). *

This is the more characteristic, as Evrat also
denounces very strongly the clergy and the bishops,
who are arrogant, and despise " le pauvre monde."
The attack on the clergy and the advocacy of
" the poor men," in combination with the legend
of *Antichrist,* cannot be a mere incident.  It is
well known that this formed the most important
book of the " Poor Men," the " Pauvres de Lyon," or
the Poor Valdenses.   The Antichrist is represented
here by the Pope, residing in Rome-Babylon.

Add to this the fact that Evrat lived in the
Champagne, and so we may presume that he himself belonged to the " Society of the Poor," which
hypothesis will be confirmed when I shall establish
the origin of the *Bible Historiale* in France.

Another point worthy of consideration is the
inversion in the order of the creation.  According
to Evrat, the animals are said to be created on the
fifth day, although the Bible fixes their creation on
the sixth day.  This is also no accident, as, curiously
enough, the order of the creation in the *Mystère du
Viel Testament* differs widely from the authorised

* Upenski, Tolkovaya Paleya, Kazan, 1876, pp. 87–88.

version. According to the *Mystère*, there were
created on the first day the four elements and the
angels; on the second, the water was separated
from the earth, and fishes and trees were created;
on the third, the sun and the moon; on the fourth
the stars; on the fifth, *the birds and animals*
(just as in Evrat), and the Paradise; on the sixth,
man.* A similar transposition of the creation
we meet also in the Slavonic version (*vide* above,
p. 28).

In the same way the other translations and texts
of versified Bibles furnish support for the existence of a *Bible Historiale* earlier than and independent of the *Historia Scholastica*, and even more
widely spread and better known than the latter,
as it formed the basis for the versifications of the
Bible.

One single legend I will further mention here, as
Bonnard cites it as an example of the invention
of the poet, whilst it is in fact an Oriental legend,
and not at all due to the inventive power of the
author.

In an anonymous versified Bible it is said that
the father of the daughters of Zelophehad† is
identical with the man who, being found gathering
sticks upon a Sabbath-day, was stoned by the con-
gregation.‡ This identification is many centuries

---

* J. de Rothschild, Le Mistére du Viel Testament, Paris, 1878, i. p. xl.
† Numbers xxvii. 1 ff.          ‡ Numbers xv. 32 ff.

older than the versification, being already mentioned in the Talmud.*

The instances cited are scanty, as I could not
here enter into details, and as the work of Bonnard
gives only small extracts. The book of Berger was
not accessible to me.

Much richer is the harvest we can gather from
the *Mystère*, which lies printed before us in the
handy edition of Baron J. de Rothschild.

In this dràmatised Bible, as we may term it,
we find again all the legends hitherto quoted in
the course of this volume. To these are also joined
many others, about which the editor says nothing,
but that "there are in these *Mystères* . . . allusions to Jewish legends not mentioned by Nicolas
de Lyra, and we do not know by what means they
came to be known by Christian writers" (i. p. x.):
"Il y a dans notre mystère . . . diverses allusions
à des legendes juives dont Nicolas de Lyre n'a pas
parlé, et nous ignorons par quelle voie elles ont été
connues des auteurs chrétiens."

The story of the creation, to begin with, is, as
we know, at variance with the Biblical. After it
follows the fall of Satan, the sin of Adam, and
the expulsion from Paradise. Here is inserted
the *Procès du Paradis* (*v.* 1295–1882), which has
no foundation whatsoever in the Bible. When God

---

* Sabbath, fol. 96b, Sifri, ed. Friedmann, fol. 33b, § 113; Talmud,
Jerush. Synhedrin, i. c. 5; Jalkut, i. §§ 743–750, fol. 228a-b.

is about to condemn mankind, a dispute arises between Justitia and Misericordia. Justitia asks for severe punishment, whilst Mercy pleads the cause of man, pointing out his weakness. The Lord then decides in favour of Mercy, and promises the salvation through His own Son.

The prototype for this heavenly drama is, as shown by the editor in the *Sepher Hayashar*, to be found also in the much older *Genesis Rabba*,* whence it has been borrowed; but what he failed to remark, and what we have already noticed here, is the identical legend in the German *Historien Bibel*. The dispute in this version is before the creation, more like the Jewish form, but the rest approaches the French, thus forming a link between these two offshoots of the old *Bible Historiale.*

We pass over smaller details; suffice it to say, that we also find here the legend of the Cross mentioned at the death of Adam, just as in the *Palæa*. Cain marries his sister Calmana, Abel Delbora, as it is told in the "Book of Jubilees." No doubt from the same source are also the names of Noah's wife and of his sons' wives, although they are not similar to the names given to them in the "Book of Jubilees." Still we must not think that this latter served as a direct source, or that it was even known to the author of the *Mystères*. The names are rather due to the prophecies of Pseudo-

* Sect. 8.

Methodius, referred to above, which were also well
known and widely spread in the old Slavonic literature.

In the *Mystère* Cain also dies, shot by Lamech ;
Nimrod builds the Tower of Babel ; Ninus appears
here together with Nimrod, as in the *Palæa* and
*Hronograf.* The death of Haran, Abraham's brother, is related as in the *Sepher Hayashar.* Haran
is thrown into the furnace and burnt to death.
The life of Joseph typifies that of Christ, as
in *Evrat,* the *Palæa,* and other Oriental writers.
Joseph's encounter with Potiphar's wife happens on
the occasion of a festival given by Pharaoh ; that
is why Potiphar and all the servants are absent
from the house. This is likewise to be found in
the above-named books. From the same source
is derived Joseph's prayer, which is shortly referred
to in the *Palæa.* Further, in the Moses episode
with the crown he tramples upon it, and so on many
parables occur till the end of the *Mystère,* which,
like the *Palæa,* concludes with Solomon, and contains a tale existing, as I have proved, only in the
*Palæa* in the older literature.

This short sketch of the contents clearly proves
that the *Mystère* is independent of the *Historia
Scholastica,* and has many a part in common with
the *Palæa,* thus pointing necessarily to another
*Bible Historiale* as its foundation, the same which
is the basis for the *Versifications.* And really such

a *Bible Historiale* seems to be preserved, but only in a copy of the fifteenth century. M. Rothschild tells us that there is in the National Library in Paris a manuscript containing almost every legendary or holy episode which has been brought on the stage as a mystery ("à peu près sans exception les épisodes sacrées ou légendaires, qui ont été transportées sur la scène,"—i. p. xi.) This manuscript has the title *Le Viel Testament lequel traicte les Histoires de la Bible, que aucuns appellent les Histoires des Hebrieux ou des Juifes*—that is, "the Old Testament which treats the histories of the Bible, called by some the histories of the Hebrews or of the Jews." This is just the title of the *Mystère*, also called *Viel Testament*, and likewise the name of the *Palæa*, the *Old Testament*, with the addition "of the Jews," and also like the title of the French manuscript—*Paläa na Judie: Palaea Secundum Judaeos.**

The French manuscript, being modern, has certainly passed through purifying hands, which eliminated as far as they could the apocryphal or other not very orthodox parts. Not so was the older text upon which the *Mystère* is directly based, differing from the former in this point. The editor says : "The differences (between the *Mystère* and the manuscript) prove sufficiently that the authors

---

* . To the *Books of the Jews* is also made reference in the Romance Chronicle. *Vide* Lespy, i. p. 19.

of the *Mystère* did not have in their hands the same version as our manuscript contains, but an older and simpler version, which did not distinguish the orthodox and the apocryphal books. This text, which may perhaps be found some day, has furnished them with the mystical comparisons between the Bible and the New Testament, in which really con-.. sisted the exegesis of the Middle Ages" (i. pp. xi., xii.)

In a few bold lines we find thus here sketched the principal features of the *Palæa*, viz., the blending together of apocryphal with canonical books, and the allegorical and mystical exegesis characteristic of the Middle Ages.

Besides the complete or ample texts, we have also an abridged *Bible Historiale* in three Romance dialects, of which two only are translations of the third, viz., a Provençal, Bearnesian, and Catalan *Bible Historiale.* -

Of these, only the last two have been published, while the Provençal is still unpublished. The Catalan has been minutely studied by Rhode,* who came to somewhat curious conclusions with regard to it. The fact that mediæval historiography begins with the Biblical narrative and joins to it later developments, had as a result that the *Palæa* was incorporated into the Russian chronicles, and that almost all mediæval chronicles

* In Suchier Denkmæler der provenzalischen Literatur u. Sprache, Halle, 1883, i. p. 589 ff.

begin their history of the world with the Bible. This misled Mr. Rhode, who took this short *Bible Historiale* for a chronicle, although it stops at Solomon, like all *Bible Historiales* we have heretofore noticed. The result to which Mr. Rhode comes may be shortly summarised as follows :—

The Romance original, from which this is a translation, belongs to the thirteenth century, and is compiled, or, better, pieced together, from six different sources, viz., (*a*) the *Vulgata* (resp. Comestor); (*b*) Apocrypha in the widest sense ; (*c*) *Elucidarium* of Honorius Augustodinensis ; (*d*) six great legends ; (*e*) the *Chronicon* of Isidorus Hispalense ; and (*f*) an unknown source.

Let us now see how far each of these sources has contributed to our compilation, and in what way. According to Mr. Rhode, the division of the history into distinct epochs is due to Isidorus's Chronicon ; but the comparison proves it to be so insufficient, that Rhode himself is compelled to acknowledge that it is only in the general outline, namely, the division into periods. This similarity is absolutely irrelevant and merely accidental, because we find precisely the same division in all other French *Bible Historiales*, as I have shown above (p. 167).

The comparison in the contents between this Romance Chronicle and the *Elucidarium* shows even more discrepancy. Out of the sixty-seven

M

columns the latter occupies in the edition of Migne, vol. clxxii., only a few traits are alike, and then we must assume that the author of the Romance Chronicle had selected them out without any visible order, a portion from here and a portion from there, never following the sequence of the *Elucidarium.* The apparent likeness comes therefore from the common source from which they have both been drawn.

What Mr. Rhode did further not succeed in showing is the source of the Apocrypha and of the six legends embodied in this supposed chronicle. He admits them simply as sources, without telling us how they penetrated to the South of France as early as the thirteenth century. The six legends are the following. The Legend of the Cross, which is very well known to us as an essential part of the *Bible Historiale,* and we need not look for Viterbo and *Beleth,* to which Mr. Rhode refers (pp. 625–626), as being similar to the form of the Chronicle. The *Denar* legend, connected with Terah, Abraham's father, has its source in the Orient, and occurs in an Oriental writer,—a fact which was not noticed by Rhode ; * and Evrat already points to the thirty silverlings when he mentions that Joseph was also sold for thirty silverlings. The further legends of Judas, Veronica, and Constantine occur very often in Slavonic literature and at an early period, so that they might also have crept into the *Bible Historiale.*

* Fabricius, Vet. Test., ii. pp. 79–81.

This view is further confirmed when we try to ascertain the *unknown source.* Two legends are taken from this, viz., a legend of Abraham, according to which Abraham destroys the idols of his father, and places the axe in the hands of the supreme idol, left undestroyed, in order to say that, for the sake of his gluttony, he killed the others, to save all the dishes for himself alone. The *source*, which was *unknown* to Mr. Rhode, is the *Sepher Hayashar*, so often quoted, and to the same source belongs also the other legend of Moses, in the well-known form, as by Herman de Valenciennes, *Palæa*, &c.

Considered as a chronicle, this book has the aspect of a mosaic pieced together in so curious a manner, that often two consecutive lines are taken from two different sources ; while considered, as I regard it, as a *Bible Historiale*, all is of one piece, of one and the same source, and corresponds entirely to other compilations belonging to the same class of works.

For in an abridged manner we find here again the principal characteristics, such as Bible history interwoven with Apocryphal tales, the mystical exegesis, and the New Testament predicted in the Old, the legend of the Cross, the chronological recapitulations, as in Herman, and also one peculiar point misunderstood hitherto. In this short *Bible Historiale*, as well as in some of the versified

Bibles, we find not unfrequently the exhortation :
"Hearken ! listen ! see !" and other similar passages.
From this the editors and Mr. Rhode presumed
that the book was read in churches and schools,
and hence the exhortation.   But if we bear in mind
that the contents is not at all orthodox, and that
the Bible in vernacular was never read in Catholic
churches, this explanation is at least a defective
one.  Quite otherwise is the meaning when we compare these phrases with the same exhortations so
frequent in the *Palœa,* to which I drew attention
when describing it.   It is a polemical work in the
Slavonic language, and addresses itself to the Jew
or other unbeliever.   In the Romance Chronicle
we have the faint echo of it.   Hence the otherwise
incomprehensible address.

Before now passing on to Italy, I will briefly
notice also the *Noble Leyczon* of the Waldenses,
consisting of a kind of short Bible history, with
expressed tendency.  To each deed or command in
the Old Testament is opposed a similar passage of
the New Testament, which proves, according to
their views, the progress and superiority of the
latter.

Our knowledge of the Italian literature is scanty.
It begins with Dante, who, as I have said, was well
acquainted with the " Legend of the Cross " and
other Apocryphal writings.  A noteworthy fact is,
further, that in Northern Italy arose the standard

book of legends, the *Legenda Aurea*, compiled out of many spurious sources by Jacobus a Voragine. A *Bible Historiale* can be proved to have existed also in Italian, although of a relatively late period. At the Council of Trent (1545–63), a book bearing the title *Fioretti . . . di tutta la Biblia . . .* was condemned as full of heretical legends. Rönsch mentions also a second book like to it, called *El Fiore di tutta la Biblia Historiato.* I regret that I have not been able to see either of them ; they are wanting even in the British Museum. But as far as I can ascertain from Fabricius,* Rönsch,† and some quotations of Wesselofsky,‡ these are likely to be nothing else than Italian *Bible Historiales*, with the same or similar Apocryphal contents. Rönsch describes it as follows : " *Both* (viz., *Fioretti* and *El Fiore*) are in the main part identical; entire chapters, especially those at the beginning, being analogous. The matter is in both the same, only slightly changed in the latter, and the number of chapters is different. The first has 137 (short) chapters, and the second 156. As far as could be ascertained at a fleeting glance, the matter was not derived directly from the 'Book of the Jubilees,' but from other books like Pseudo-Methodius; and from our comparison with regard to the legends of Adam, they seem to be in nearer

* Vet. Test., ii. 122 ; *cf.* i. 864.
† Das Buch der Jubiläen, Leipzig, 1874, p. 469.
‡ Razyskaniya, x. p. 377, No. 4.

relation to the *Gadela Adam* (*Vita Adami*), translated from the Ethiopic, than to the 'Book of the
Jubilees.' "

To this description we add that given by Fabricius, who says that it contains the history from
the creation down to the time of Christ. It is full
of absurd legends, and those relative to Christ are
very much akin to the Apocryphal Gospels of the
Infancy.

In the life of Adam there is also a reference to
the "Legend of the Cross," according to the quota-
tion of Wesselofsky.

Thus we have here the principal elements con-
stituting the *Bible Historiale*, the legendary history similar to the " Book of the Jubilees," though
only through the mediation of Pseudo-Methodius, just as in the *Mystère*, &c., legends of the
Biblical personages, .Adam, and the Cross, and
the apocryphal Infancy tales, occurring also in
some of the versified French *Bible Historiales*.
We may now fairly admit the existence of a *Bible
Historiale* in Italy, independent of the *Historia
Scholastica*, and nearer to the *Palæa*. Here also
I must leave to others the fuller inquiry.

It remains now to pursue the *Bible Historiale*
in the German literature also. More than forty
manuscripts were studied by Merzdorf,* the editor

* T. Merzdorf, Historienbibel, vol. c. and ci. of Literarischer Verein,
Stuttgard.

of the German *Historien Bibel*, and yet the material is far from being exhausted. This proves the great favour that book enjoyed in Germany, and consequently the great influence it exercised. More than one literary point, however, is left unsettled. In his valuable introduction, Merzdorf classifies the different extant versions, and comes to the conclusion that there are two distinct classes of *Bible Historiales* falsely united under the same title. One is entirely dependent on the *Historia Scholastica* of Comestor, and the other is more or less a prose transcription of Rudolf von Ems's Chronicle. It is now established * that the *Historia Scholastica* was early translated into French (*c.* 1286 or 1289) by a certain Guiars de Moulin, canon of St. Peter's in Aire (Aëria), near the frontier of Flanders, and upon this version the later French *Bible Historiale* is based. This was also translated and widely circulated in Germany, and forms Group I., edited by Merzdorf as the real *Historien Bibel.* As such, we have nothing to do with it.

Besides this, Group II. is subdivided by Merzdorf into two branches (*a*) and (*b*), the first corresponding entirely to the Chronicle of Rudolf, the other, less complete, but more amplified, belonging, as he asserts, to a later development of that chronicle, due to another anonymous author.

---

* Reusz, in Herzog, Real Encyclopædie, xiii. p. 30 ff. *s. v.* Romanische Bibelübersetzung.

We will deal shortly with IIa. It is not my purpose to enter now into the vexed question as to the priority of the versified to the prosaical form, in so far as it regards mediæval literature. I, for my own part, strongly believe that every artificial poem is based upon a prose original and not *vice versâ;* and thus this falsely termed chronicle is only the Bible history from the creation to the time of Solomon, exactly like the *Palæa*, the work of Herman of Valenciennes, &c.; and is no doubt based upon a prose original. Hence the apparent identity of the present prose version IIa. with the poem, which is explained as a transcription of that metrical form. It may be that this latter exercised some influence upon the present text, but the comparison with the other literatures shows that we may assume a prose original for the poem of Rudolf of Ems.

It is a remarkable fact that almost all the productions of this poet are more or less based upon foreign or Oriental themes; it is so with " Barlaam and Josaphat," the Oriental tale of Buddha, and with the "War of Troy," for the first time treated in French by Benoît de St. Maur, but before unknown in the West; and, finally, with the "Good Gerhard of Köln," the Oriental origin of which I proved some years ago. It is therefore not unjustifiable to presume also a foreign and prose original for his chronicle also.

Unfortunately the poem is not printed, and we

are reduced to draw our information from the pamphlet published in 1839 by Vilmar, who was the first to devote a special inquiry to the subject. The conclusion he arrived at was, that Rudolf is dependent upon Comestor, but only in a remote way, and he may have also made use of the *Pantheon* of Godfrey of Viterbo and Solinus' *Polyhistor* (Vilmar, p. 13). That is to say, that the Chronicle of Rudolf bears some resemblance to the above-mentioned, without being a *verbal* copy of them, as is the case with the Bible history of Group I.; thus the chronicle has the same characteristic features as the French and Romance *Bible Historiales* which we have previously studied, and might rightly also be termed *Bible Historiale*. Moreover, it cannot be assumed, as some might be induced to think, that Rudolf borrowed from the *Speculum Historiale* of Vincentius of Beauvais, as his chronicle was finished *c.* 1251, whilst the latter composed his *Speculum* after 1254.

The same mistake which induced Rhode to call the *Romance Bible Historiale* "Chronicle" induced the German writers to give the same name to the poem of Rudolf, which does not extend farther than to the time of Solomon, in a manner identical with that of all the other *Bible Historiales* and the *Palæa*. But, like the literary development of Byzantium, where Malalas or Hamartolos or other chroniclers incorporated the history of the Biblical period into their chronicle, joining the later world history to the end of the Biblical, so it happened in Germany and Russia also, where the chronicles began with the *Palæa* resp., with its German counterpart, the versified Bible of Rudolf of Ems. Hence the misleading name, which I hope will soon be dispensed with.

Richer in details, and better known by some extracts, is version II*b.*, which is also considered as a transliteration of a poem into a prose composition based upon a development of Rudolf's Bible, due to an anonymous author. This more amplified version is called the *Christ Herre* version, after the beginning words, whilst Rudolf's is distinguished as the *Richter Gott* version, after the two initial words. According to Vilmar, this II*b.* is nothing else than a literal translation of Comestor's *Historia Scholastica* and the *Pantheon* of Godfrey of Viterbo.

But if we are to believe the assertion of Merzdorf, that II*b.* represents exactly that unpublished poem, then matters stand quite otherwise. Among the manuscripts of II*b.* there are some true *Bible Historiales.* To these belongs also a MS., once in possession of a certain Mr. Schröder, who gives the following description of it. "The MS. is a copy from *c.* 1430–50, whose author might have lived in the thirteenth century (that is, contemporaneously with Rudolf!). It contains an abstract of the Biblical history down to the Maccabeans, without the Prophets and Psalms. The text is not couched after the *Vulgata,* but is probably taken from an older German codex." *

What especially strikes us here is, that the text of the Bible is not translated from the Vulgate, but that it is due to some other source—the author presumes a German version without any proof. It is not necessary to add that this Bible history is full of legends, apocryphal and otherwise.

A similar manuscript of the fifteenth century, with illustrations, is noted by Von der Hagen, who published the complaint of Adam after his expulsion from Paradise in a wording like to the legend of Adam in the *Palœa,* &c., and a parallel to it from the above manuscript.

Mr. Merzdorf, who numbered this manuscript, and also arranged it amongst those of II*b.,* unfortunately considered the legendary parts to be irrelevant, and omitted them entirely, being satisfied only with a few remarks. He did not pay any great attention to this smaller group generally, as it was of secondary importance to him, although a better inquiry would have disclosed to him the real value of this version.

There still remains a third manuscript belonging to the same group, once in possession of a certain J. D. Müller, afterwards in that of the Pastor Goetze, famous through his controversies with Les-

* Merzdorf, pp. 34–35.

sing, and at present in the municipal library of
Hamburg. Out of this manuscript, also from the
fifteenth century (*c.* 1458), Müller gave some extracts of the creation reproduced by Fabricius,[*]
enabling us thus to recognise the relationship between these manuscripts and the *Bible Historiale.*

The history begins with the dispute between
Mercy and Justice, as in the French *Mystery.*
The mystical parallelism between the Old and
New Testament is consistently pursued throughout the history. Very detailed is the description
of the angels who fell, during three days and three
nights, from heaven into hell. The rank and order
of the angels is explicitly stated. The description of
how the world and Adam were created follows, and
it is said that Adam fell into a deep slumber, wherein
he saw prophetical visions telling him of the future
redemption. During this time Eve was created, not
by God Himself, but by an angel. Here the author
mentions the Jewish legend that Adam had had
another wife, created, like him, out of loam and
outside Paradise, while Eve was created from his
rib in Paradise. The legend referred to is well
known in Jewish literature, and appears in the
*Alfabetum Pseudo-Siracidicum* (*cir.* eighth century).[†]

The *Bible Historiale* goes on to say that the

---

[*] Vet. Test., i. 36–47.
[†] Ed. Steinschneider, Berlin, 1858, f. 23*a*.

serpent which deceived Eve was Lucifer, and the serpent walked upright and had a woman's head. After the sin Adam and Eve repented of it by a severe penitence in the waters of Gihon. This episode corresponds exactly with the version published by Von der Hagen. We are told also that Cain was born together with his sister Calmana, and Abel with Delbora, whom he marries afterwards, just as in the Mystery and Pseudo-Methodius.

Amply developed are the death of Adam and the legend of the Cross, intimately connected with it. Seth goes to the gates of Paradise to bring food for his sick father. The angel Michael appears, and tells him that 5200 years must elapse before the sin of Adam will be atoned, and then God's Son will come with the oil of mercy. Seven days after Adam dies, and also Eve ; all as in the similar legend in the *Palæa, Mystère*, &c., drawn from the same apocryphal source.

The extract given by Fabricius stops here, but it suffices to show that we have before us a work quite analogous to the *Bible Historiale* described above.

Naturally the more modern a copy is the more probable it is that it was influenced by other similar works, as, for instance, the *Historia Scholastica*. But, nevertheless, all the characteristic features have been preserved, and point to another independent and certainly older source.

One point (which we reserved for the last) in the

description of this German *Bible Historiale* is of
the highest importance, as it will enable us to find
the connecting link between this and the Slavonic
version, viz., "When God was going to create heaven
and earth, He *created first the angel Satael*, and
afterwards the other angels." This *Satael* is nobody
else than the *Satanael* of the *Palœa*, occurring
only in Bogomilian writings, and due solely to their
heretical influence. In perfect harmony with this
is also the presumption that *Satanael* was the first
being created, the most powerful, and superior to
the other angels, whence his arrogance and fall.

Curiously enough, *Satanael* is also mentioned in
the *Historia Scholastica* of Comestor, where he is
identified with Lucifer, but falsely explained as
*Satan : adversary—El : to God* (sic dictus est ante
lapsum, vel forte post lapsum, *Satan*, quasi *adver-
sarius, El : Deo* (Glosse to Genesis, c. iv.) This
brings us to the question as to the origin of the
*Bible Historiale* in France, and also to the other
question, whence did Comestor draw the materials
for his *Historia Scholastica*, especially that which
regards the Biblical legends? I cannot enter here
into this difficult question in any detailed manner.

As sources, Comestor himself mentions, among
others, Methodius and Josephus. The former is,
as I have proved, a compilation of the "Book of
the Jubilees ;" and as to Josephus, it is remarkable
that many a legend professedly taken from his

works is not to be found in them ; so, for instance, the story of Potiphar is nowhere to be found in Josephus, although contained in the *Jerusalem Targum* (Genesis xxxix. 1) and in the *Talmud.*\* Then the story of Moses's two marvellous rings, and that Cain married his sister Calmana, said to be taken from Josephus, is really from Methodius, and so forth.

On the other hand, a comparison with the old French versified Bibles, and even the German, shows, notwithstanding great discrepancies, a similarity which cannot be denied, and which can only be explained by admitting a common source. It ought not to be forgotten that these latter also very often refer to Josephus and Hieronymus, although they certainly never made direct use of their works. Noteworthy is the same fact in the *Palæa*, where Josephus is also avowedly quoted, and here, also, surely through the mediation of some other work.

The source for the Western *Bible Historiale*, and in some way for the *Historia Scholastica*, is therefore to be sought in the Greeko-Slavonic *Palæa*, brought by currents, we shall soon learn, from the East into France and Provence.

One of the striking features is the free admission of apocrypha and their blending together in one *Bible*. These apocrypha do not appear *before* that

* Tractat Sotah, f. 13*b*.

period in the West, with the exception of England, where the *Evangelium Nicodemi* seems to have penetrated very early (eighth or ninth century), but which exercised no influence upon the surrounding literatures.

The Infancy Gospels are also of a recent date. Herman of Valenciennes, who was the first to versify the Bible, was also the first who versified the Gospels. Comestor did not know them; only a century later they were inserted in the *Speculum* of Vincentius.*

Not in orthodox, but in heterodox circles did the Apocryphal literature have its rise and development; and here also arose the *Bible Historiale*, whose appearance coincided strangely with a remarkable movement which took place at that time in France and throughout the centre of Europe.

At the beginning of the thirteenth century arose a society in Metz for the purpose of reading the Bible in the vernacular. Till that time the Bible was only known in the Latin translation of Hieronymus, being thus accessible only to the clergy, while the people were absolutely ignorant of it. The result of the reading and understanding the Bible was that the members of that society soon began to despise the priests and the bishops, whose deeds and doctrines did not at all harmonise with the teaching

---

* R. Rheinsch, die Pseudoevangelien in d. rom. u. germ. Literatur, Halle, 1879, pp. 7, 16–18.

of the Bible. The Bishop of Metz immediately denounced the society to Pope Innocent III., who first allowed the reading of the Bible in the vernacular, as there was no law which forbade it. The gap between the clerics and laymen consequently widened more and more, and threatened to become irreparable. This could never be in the interest of the Church; so the Bishop remonstrated energetically against it to the Pope, urging the adoption of a speedy remedy, as the members of the Bible-reading society rebelled also against the authority of the Pope himself. Innocent being compelled to do something in the matter, appointed a commission, consisting of the Bishop of Metz, the Abbot of Cistercium, and three other Abbots, to investigate it, and to examine the proceedings of that society.

The result was that the members of the Bible-reading society were convicted of being *heretics and their Bible was pronounced full of heretical contents.* In consequence thereof the society was dissolved and the Bible *burnt.* With this fact begins the persecution of the Bible in the vernacular by the Catholic Church, which finally decreed the prohibition of reading the Bible in the vernacular at the Council held at Toulouse in the year 1229. After this no layman dared read the Bible unless in Latin.*

This early date proves that at the beginning of

---

* Neander, Kirchengeschichte, 4th ed., Gotha, 1864, vol. viii. pp. 37-42.

the thirteenth century the Bible must have been widely circulated and eagerly read in the vernacular. Indeed, the translated Bible read by the society in Metz was an *imported* one, brought thither by the *Waldenses,* as is expressly stated.*

We are thus in possession of the link which connects the translation of the Bible into the vernacular and the circulation of it, with the heretical sects flourishing about that time, especially in the South of France.

There is now every evidence to prove the existence of such a translation, and the profound knowledge of it amongst the heretical sects, said by all the contemporary writers to be very well versed in the Bible.

This is a common characteristic for every dissenting movement which appears in the history of religion, and especially of the Christian Church. The separation is based upon and supported by the real or pretended better understanding of Holy Scripture. Without going into further details, already *Petrus Siculus,* speaking of the Paulicians in Asia Minor, asserts that even before their emigration from Armenia they possessed a translation of the Bible, and that their women were well acquainted with its contents. *Cedrenus* adds that they brought it with them, coming into the Byzantine empire.

* Neander, *l. c.*

That the Slavonians had the Bible translated at an early period has been often enough stated in these pages. In the year 1007 the heretical sects in the Occident were already accused of reading the Old and New Testament, only with polemical purposes, and with the intention of denying the truth therein contained. And finally, *Reinerius,* who is the chief source for our knowledge about the Albigenses, states that almost every heretic in the twelfth and thirteenth centuries knew at least the New Testament by heart in the vernacular.* And they not only knew the Bible in the vernacular, but also taught that the translated Bible had the same power as the Latin Bible.†

Internal evidence proves further that the oldest French Bible was not translated from the *Vulgate,* but from a *Greek* original, or from another which in its turn was translated from the Greek version of the LXX. One at least of the German texts—the others have not yet been studied from this point of view—is not derived from the Vulgate, but from another text, supposed by Schröder to be an older German ; but this, lastly, is also not more than a translation, and a different one from the Vulgate.

The literary and missionary activity of the Albigenses is too well established to be doubted. We

* Faber, Waldenses, p. 400, No. 1, and p. 492.

† C. U. Hahn, Geschichte der Ketzer im Mittelalter, Stuttgart, 1845, vol. i. p. 94.

find already in 1025 the record of their schools,
where they taught their doctrines and expounded
the Bible.* The same Reinerius tells us that the
*Cathari* had more schools than the theologians,
and his own words are : "In almost every locality
in Lombardy, Provence, and other places, their
number exceeded by far that of the theologians,
and they had more pupils, who disputed openly and
induced the people to enter into discussions with
them ; and they preached in tents and fields, and
nobody dared stop them, as they had powerful and
numerous protectors. In the diocese of Padua alone
they had more than forty-one schools, not counting
those of Germany and France." †

At the same time the translation of the Bible
into the vernacular was undertaken by Petrus
Valdo (*c.* 1170), founder of the sect of the Waldenses, who is said to have paid two priests—
*Stephan de Ansa* and *Bernhard Ydras*—for their
work, as at his command they translated the
Gospels and other Biblical books into the Romance
language.‡ Soon afterwards (1179), that is, only
*eight* years later, a deputation of the Waldenses
waited upon the Pope, Alexander III., during the
time when a Council was held in Rome, with the
object of obtaining his approbation for a French
translation of the Psalms with glosses, and several

---

* Faber, *l. c.*, p. 358 ff.                    † Ibid., *l. c.*, p. 361.
‡ Neander, *l. c.*, viii. p. 409 ; Faber, p. 456.

other parts of the Old and of the New Testament. *Gualterus Mapes,* who gives a graphic description of their appearance, was also appointed to discuss with them concerning their dogmas. The result was a scornful dismissal of their demand.*

There is no doubt, as is expressly stated, that the dismissed translation was not at all literal, but was amplified by *glosses,* that is, it was a paraphrastic translation.† Further noteworthy is the difference in the *wording* when the New and when the Old Testament is spoken of. The Old Testament is never mentioned *entirely;* only *parts* of it are translated, whilst generally the Gospels are wholly translated. This is easily explained when we bear in mind the form of the *Bible Historiale,* that the translation confined itself to the *historical parts,* leaving out the rest, and therefore is only spoken of *parts* of the Bible.

If we might draw a conclusion from the contemporary Jewish literature, the character of this paraphrastic Bible, or Bible with explanatory glosses, might have been somewhat similar to the text of the Bible together with the Commentary of R. Salomo Itzhaki (Rashi), who lived in Troyes, and died 1105, with the single difference that here all is written in Hebrew, while in the former case

* Faber, *l. c.,* p. 471.

† " Qui librum Domino Papæ præsentaverunt *lingua conscriptum gallica* in quo textus et *glossa* Psalterii plurimorumque Legis utriusque librorum continebatur."

all is translated. This Commentary, which may be considered as consisting of glosses to the Biblical text, is full of legendary explanations, drawn from the old Aggadic literature, and the influence it exercised even upon the Christian commentators is pretty well shown by the example of *Nicolas de Lyra*, who is greatly indebted to Rashi.

It is not my intention to follow out here the friendly relations which existed between the Jews and the heretical sects in France, and how far they mutually borrowed from each other. Suffice it to say, that many a zealous priest of the Catholic Church complained bitterly about this free intercourse.*

Returning to the Bible of the Waldenses and of the other sects, its contents must have been amplified by glosses of a legendary character, and no doubt contrasting with the dogmas of the ruling Church, as the Council of Metz declared it to be *heretical*, and condemned it to the pile.

This points clearly to our *Bible Historiale*, whose prominent peculiarity is the adoption to so large an extent of apocryphal tales and legends, which constitute its chief elements.

The diffusion of the apocryphal literature in Europe is due in a certain measure to the activity of the heretical sects, originating especially in the Middle Ages in Bulgaria, with which country they

* Neander, *l. c.*, viii. p. 43 ff.

never lost connection. Thence they also carried this literature to the West, and it is by no means an exaggeration to presume the original identity of the Western *Bible Historiale* with the *Palæa*.

The coincidence of so many facts brought under consideration is so striking, that there cannot be any other explanation for it than to assume the former unity, preserved even through the manifold changes which the *Bible Historiale* underwent in course of time and in different countries. The main features remained, and we have been able to trace the existence of such a *Bible Historiale* back to the twelfth century as the basis for the versified Bible, for the *Mystère*, and for the abbreviation in the three Romance dialects of Bearn, Provence, and Catalonia.

The crusade against the Albigenses broke down the poetical life of Provence, and at the same time stamped out every trace of the heretical literature. What wonder that the *Bible Historiale* suffered the fate encountered by all similar works. But the influence could not be totally obliterated, and even in the orthodox disguise we could recognise the old *Bible Historiale*.

.   .   .   .   .   .   .

Merely as an additional remark, for it leaves a wide field for conjecture and special studies, I venture to give an explanation of the name of that illustrated Bible commonly called *Bible of the Poor*.

Up to the present day nobody has succeeded in either tracing the origin of that Bible or in explaining its name. Berjeau, if I am not mistaken, is the last who devoted a study to this question. (The later publication of Laib and Schwarz deals merely with the windows of Hirschau and the German texts of the *Biblia Pauperum*). He describes the *Biblia Pauperum* as follows :—

"The *Biblia Pauperum* is a set in the first edition of forty, and in the second of fifty woodcuts, disposed in three horizontal compartments, which we will call upper, middle, and lower, each being itself arranged in three vertical divisions, which may be distinguished as left, centre, and right, all divided from each other by an architectural framework, uniform alternately for all the *verso* and *recto* pages of the work.

"The left division of the upper compartment contains a number of lines (which are not rhythmical) in black letter, with very contracted abbreviations, in which the subject of the Old Testament immediately under is explained in few words, with a reference to the centre subject, taken from the New Testament.

"The right division contains likewise the explanation of the subject on the right, with its reference to the same subject of the New Testament represented in the centre of the page.

"The centre vertical division of the upper compartment represents a double window, with a prophet on each side of a central pillar. The name of the prophet is inscribed under his bust, which generally holds the end of a scroll, on which is written some sentence from that prophet, referring to the central subject.

"The middle horizontal compartment, with its three vertical divisions, forms the principal part of the woodcut, the left and right subjects being taken from the Old Testament, while the central subject is always taken from the New Testament; this latter only being in chronological order.

" The lower compartment contains, like the upper one, in the centre, in a double window, the busts of two prophets, each holding a scroll, with his name and a sentence taken from his prophecies, and referring to the centre subject. In the blank spaces on each side is a leonine verse explaining the subject above ; while at the bottom of the page, immediately under the busts of the prophets, is another leonine verse explaining the central design." *

In order to make it clearer, I here give the trans-lated contents of leaf v.

" *The Holy Family in Egypt.*—Upper com-partment, left. "We read in the thirty-first and thirty-third chapters of Exodus that when Moses had come to the foot of Mount Sinai, he alone ascended the mountain to receive the Law ; and when he had done this and was descending, he saw the molten calf which Aaron had made of gold. Moses himself having thrown away the Tables, destroyed the calf and broke it up ; which well figured the idols falling in a heap when Christ entered Egypt."

Next to it the double window ; at the left is the bust of the Prophet Hosea, with the inscription : ' He shall break down (their altars),' taken from Hosea x. 2. In the next window, to the right, is Nahum with the scroll : ' Out of the house of thy gods will I cut off the graven image and the molten image ' (Nahum i. 14). The next white square, forming the upper right compartment, con-

* Berjeau, Biblia Pauperum, London, 1859, pp. 3-4.

tains the following passage : 'We read in the first
book of Samuel (chap. v.) that the Philistines had
placed the ark of the Lord, that they had taken in
war, near Dagon, their god. Those who entered
the temple in the morning found Dagon lying on
the ground, and both his hands broken off : which
figure was truly fulfilled when the Blessed Virgin
came with Christ, her child, into Egypt; then
the idols of Egypt fell into a heap ; and it figures
the Virgin, who with Christ enters the state
of trial into which infidels through error have
collapsed.'

The middle is occupied by the three designs
described, and underneath the lower compartment
contains on the left front the leonine verse : 'By
Moses the sacred image of the calf was destroyed.'
Then the bust of Zachariah, with the inscription :
'I will cut off the names of the idols out of the
earth' (Zach. xiii. 2). Next to it is the bust of
Zephaniah, with the words : 'The Lord will famish
all the gods of the earth' (Zeph. ii. 11). Above it
is the other leonine verse, explaining the design :
'The ark is made the cause of the sudden ruin of
Dagon.' And finally, at the bottom of the page,
just under the lower double window, and thus
under the design of the centre, is the third leonine
verse : 'The idols fell swiftly when Christ was
present.'"

Berjeau says further : " It would not be easy to

ascertain who was the author of the *Biblia Paupe-rum*, who conceived the idea of such a book, and who composed the three lines of poetry which explain the three subjects on each page. The rest of the text contained on both sides of the upper compartment is not rhythmical, as it has been said, but contains mere quotations from the Old Testament and Prophets with reference to the central subject taken from the New Testament." * Nevertheless, Berjeau † suggests that Vincentius of Beauvais might be the author of the text, on no other ground than that he is now acknowledged to be the author of the *Speculum Humanæ Salvationis*, which was likewise engraved and printed by the xylographer of Haarlem to whom the engravings of the *Biblia Pauperum* are attributed.

But before we enter into the study of this, for us, most important point, we will deal shortly with the history of this *Biblia Pauperum*, its date, and the origin of the drawings.

" It is pretty certain that the author or copyist of this text was not the artist who made the designs. The circumstance that there are sensible variations between the drawing of the subject and its Latin explanations shows sufficiently that the artist did not understand the literal meaning of the Latin text." ‡ This text belongs, therefore, to an earlier period, and the original manuscript may be traced

* *Loc. cit.*, p. 5.     † *Loc. cit.*, p. 23.     ‡ *Loc. cit.*, p. 5.

to the twelfth or thirteenth century, as the leonine
verse and the abbreviations used in the text point
clearly to that period.

The costumes of the block-book announce a more
recent period, namely, 1410–20. The conclusion
at which Berjeau arrives as to the time when this
first block-book arose, and the circumstances to
which it owes its origin, is : ‡ " By its architectural
framework our block-book may be said to belong
to the Tuscan school, as illustrated in the Duomo
di Orvieto, in Santa Maria di Toscanella, in San
Ministo di Firenze. The drawings, imitated from
the fresco paintings of Italian convents, most likely
by John van Eyck, ornamented some costly MS.
before being engraved on wood by some of the
*figuersnyders* so numerous in the Netherlands at
the end of the fourteenth and the beginning of the
fifteenth century. The block-book was afterwards
the model on which were made and painted the
windows of the celebrated Convent of Hirschau,
and was the starting-point of numberless imita-
tions by the early German painters and wood and
metal engravers, such as Springinklee, Albert Dürer,
Schäuffelein, Hans Hemmling, &c."

Other reproductions of later periods have sometimes
changed these drawings. I will not attempt here
to enter into the difficult and unsettled question as
to the origin of those Italian wall-paintings which

* *Loc. cit.*, p. 11.

served as a model for the block-book. How did this kind of picture arise just in a place and in a time at which a strong religious, or more properly heterodox, movement was prevalent in that country? How was it that it was just there that art for the first time emancipated itself from the official Byzantine influence? Tischendorf has dwelt at length on another very interesting point, viz., when and how far did the *apocryphal* tales creep into the Christian art of painting? Traces of this are also extant in our block-book; for instance, on folio 2, where the *ox* and *ass* are drawn standing near the crib in which Christ is lying, though no mention is made of them in the Gospels. They are derived from the apocryphal Gospel of Infancy. Or on folio 6, the story of the fall of the idols in Egypt, related above, and so forth.

This and other similar questions must be left for the moment undecided, and so also the question as to whether there was not an illustrated block-book or MS. older than that now known, and which underwent the same refinement and change through John van Eyck as was effected in the case of his drawings by his followers.

There is no doubt, however, that the original text is much older; and yet some have tried to explain the name *Biblia Pauperum*, or *Bible of the Poor*, as the name given to the block-book, which was naturally cheaper than the illustrated MS.,

and therefore termed the "Bible of the Poor," as
every man was enabled to buy it. But whoever
is acquainted, however slightly, with the prices such
works fetched in the fifteenth and sixteenth centuries would immediately recognise that even in
the shape of a block-book such a book was by far
too dear to be bought by a poor man. The name
must be, therefore, of quite a different origin, and
was surely the name of the *text* itself, which is a
kind of abridged Bible, and served as a basis for
the later or contemporary drawings.

Indeed, if we look more accurately into this text,
we again find the elements of the *Bible Historiale*,
with the same characteristic opposition of the Old
to the New Testament, and fulfilment in the latter
of the predictions given in the former. What is
more, out of *eighty* texts which form the forty pages,
two in the upper compartment of each page, not
less than *seventy-six* are taken from the Old Testament, and especially from the following books :—
Twenty-one from Genesis (fol. 1, 5, 8, 10 *bis*, 12,
16, 17 *bis*, 18, 23, 24, 25, 26, 27, 30, 32, 33, 34,
38, 39); six from Exodus (2, 6, 9, 18, 26, 35);
one from Leviticus (4); four from Numbers (2, 9,
13, 25); one from Deuteronomy (38); four from
Judges (28, 29, 33); twelve from Samuel (3, 4, 5,
6, 7, 8, 13, 14, 16, 21, 28, 37); fourteen from Kings
(3, 7, 11 *bis*, 14, 19 *bis*, 22, 23, 24, 34, 35, 36,
37); two from Jonah (27, 29); three from Daniel

(12, 22, 31) ; three from Song of Solomon (30, 31, 40) ; one from Ezra (15) ; one from Esther (36) ; one from Job (39) ; two from Maccabees (15, 21) ; whilst from the New Testament there are one from Matthew (20) ; one from Luke (32) ; and two from the Apocalypse (20, 40).

From this proportion we see that *all the texts, without any exception,* are taken from the *historical books* of the Bible only, like those of which the *Bible Historiale* is composed, and *none* from the Prophets.

The text itself closely resembles that examined by us as the *Bible Historiale.* Thus we again find here the identification of Joseph with Christ. Joseph is further sold for *thirty pieces of silver,* which clearly denotes that the author did not take the passage directly from the canonical Bible, but from an uncanonical source, here the *Bible Historiale.* The quotations are also never literal, but are rather contractions of the Holy Writ, just as they are to be found in the above-named book.

To these internal evidences as to the origin of this *short Bible* is also added the name it bears as *Biblia Pauperum.*

The Waldenses were best known under the name of the *Poor of Lyons* (*Pauperes Lugdunenses*). Under this name they appeared at the Council in Rome, and under the same name they became famous for centuries.

Many a common point between their Bible and their *Noble Leyczon* induces me to ascribe to them also the authorship of this short Biblical treatise, perhaps from the beginning already accompanied with rough sketches, out of which arose the later more refined drawings. And so it got the name of *Biblia Pauperum,* or the "Bible of the Poor," viz., the Bible of *the Poor of Lyons,* preserved as such until the present time.

It is not without interest to notice that nearly all the first block-books deal with subjects favoured in the highest degree by the heretical sects, and became popular books. Thus the *Antichrist,* the *Legend of the Cross,* the *Apocalypse of St. John,* are among the oldest block-books, all containing subjects with which we have become familiar in the course of these pages.

The identification of the *Poor* with the Waldenses, or the *Poor of Lyons,* is not only not far-fetched, as it might seem at the first glance, but is also the only plausible explanation of the title, as it explains at the same time the origin of the book.

# APPENDIX B.

## THE ORIGIN OF THE GLAGOLITIC ALPHABET.

DOBROVSKY, the founder of Slavonic philology, at the close of the last century for the first time drew attention to a mode of writing employed in some Slavonic books totally different from the Cyrillian. This question was vigorously taken up by Kopitar when he published in 1836 the Slavonic text written with such characters, and known thenceforth under the name of "*Glagolita Clozianus.*" The problem which presented itself thus to the students of Slavonic philology was to ascertain the date and the probable origin of this long-forgotten or totally neglected alphabet.

The most opposite views were taken upon the matter, and a discussion ensued which lasted nearly half a century, till at least one point was generally agreed upon, viz., the greater age of the Glagolitic alphabet and its priority to the Cyrillian.

The reasons brought forward are twofold : philological and palæographical. A close inquiry into the nature of the language represented by the Glago-

O

litic texts proves it to be of the most archaic form,
and to approach as closely as possible that language which is considered by Professor Miklosich
to be the basis of the so-called Church Slavonic
or Old Slavonic language—the Slavonic dialect,
namely, into which the Apostles Cyril and Method
are said to have translated the Bible for the first
time.   In these Glagolitic texts are thus preserved
the oldest specimens of the Slavonic literature,
whilst the language of the Cyrillian text is more
modern, and already contains traces of dialectic
influences, chiefly Bulgarian peculiarities, as is
only natural, when we remember the rise and development of the Slavonic literature in Bulgaria.
Among these texts we do not find anything of
so hoar an antiquity as some of the Glagolitica
possess, where one or another is considered to be
no more than a hundred years distant from the
lifetime of the apostles.

So far the philological reason.   To this the palæographical now comes as a powerful support.   Just
as we find in the West of Europe *palimpsests*,
that is, parchments which have been written upon
twice, the first writing having been erased, so we
find them in the Slavonic literature, and the peculiar thing is, that the *first* writing has always been a
Glagolitical, which was erased and a *new* Cyrillian
text written upon it.   Never up to the present day
has the contrary been discovered.   We know of no

instance in which a Glagolitical text has been written upon a primitive Cyrillian.

For these two reasons the Glagolitza, as we will in future term this alphabet, calling the other Cyrillitza, is now universally accepted to be the older alphabet, superseded in a later period by a more modern, which usurped its name, and not the opposite of this, as was formerly believed. The palimpsests also show that the Cyrillian writers had Glagolitical texts at hand.

The next question is *the origin* of this alphabet. Is it a primitive one or a derived ? and if the latter, whence is it derived, and on what model is it formed ?

My purpose is here only to enter into the discussion of the origin of the Glagolitza, and not into the history and development of the Glagolitic literature, that is, of the works written and published in these characters. I confine myself to the characters themselves, to point out their peculiarity, endeavouring to give a new solution to this oft discussed problem.

We have to consider first the *forms* of the letters, and then the order in which they are arranged. Of minor importance, and yet still important, are the curious names the letters of this alphabet possess. The difficulty of explaining the names and the order of the Cyrillitza, as these are identical with the Glagolitza, was no less in former

times when the Glagolitza was unknown. Moreover, the form of some letters of the Cyrillian
alphabet was puzzling, as their origin could not
easily be traced.

As regards this alphabet, it is now proved that
the main part of it was taken from the Greek uncial
writing, and the signs employed for sounds strange
to the Greek are due to the Glagolitza, whence
they were borrowed by the later compiler of this
alphabet, who, as it seems to be, was St. Clemens
(† 916) in Bulgaria, for in his biography it is
expressly stated "that he invented other clearer
letters than those which were invented by the
wise Cyrill" (ἐσοφίσατο καὶ χαρακτῆρας ἑτέρους γραμ-
μάτων πρὸς τὸ σαφέστερον ἤ οὕς ἐξεῦρεν ὁ σοφός
Κύριλλος).* The Greek literature and the Greek
writing were generally known in Bulgaria at that
period, and it was only natural to adopt the better
known signs for their own language than to adopt
an entirely new alphabet, as the Glagolitic was,
taking from this only the signs not wanting in the
Greek alphabet,—just as was done many centuries before, under the same circumstances and
at the same spot—in Bulgaria—by Bishop Ulfilas
when he invented the so-called Gothic alphabet.

Not so, however, with the order and the names
of the letters ; *they* were both transferred from one

---

* Miklosich, Algemeine Encyclopædie, Ersch und Gruber, vol. lxviii.
1859, p. 413.

to the other ; the Glagolitza was changed into the Cyrillitza with respect only to what belongs to the form ; the rest remained unchanged. The letters of the alphabet serve further as ciphers indicating the numbers, the value depending upon the place the letter occupies in the alphabet. By this numerical value attributed to the letters the order of the alphabet has been maintained.

More complete than the Cyrillitza is the Glagolitza, which numbers forty signs, as the plate at the end of the book shows. There are the forms of both alphabets, together with others to which I shall refer hereafter.

I now give the name of every letter, with its translation, numerical value, and pronunciation, indicating at the same time which letter does not exist in the Cyrillitza and *vice versa*. The number assigned to them corresponds entirely with the number in the plate, and is the same as that adopted by Kopitar and Miklosich :—

1. azŭ : ego, 1, a.
2. bukŭvi : littera, 2, b.
3. vêdê : scio, 3, v.
4. glagoli : loquere, 4, g.
5. dobro : bonum, 5, d.
6. esti : est, 6, e.
7. živête : vivite, 7, ž (English j).
8. zêlo : valde, 8, dz.
9. zemiya : terra, 9, z.
10. iže : qui, 10, i.
11. i       20, i.

12. dya        30, dy (only Glagol.)
13. kako: quomodo, 40, k.
14. lyudiye : homines, 50, l.
15. myislete : cogitate, 60, m.
16. naši : noster, 70, n.
17. onŭ : ille, 80, o.
18. pokoy : quies, 90, p.
19. rĭci : dic, 100, r.
20. slovo : verbum, 200, s.
21. tvrŭdo : durum, 300, t.
22. ukŭ : doctrina (?), 400, u.
23. frŭtŭ        500, f (ph).
24. chêrŭ :        600, h.
25. otŭ : ab, 700, ō.
26. šta        800, št (sht).
27. ci        900, c (tz).
28. črŭvi : vermis, 1000, č (ch).
29. ša :        š (sh).
30. yerŭ :        ŭ (a dull sound).
31. yerŭy : .        ŭy.
32. yerĭ :        ĭ.
33. êti        ê (a kind of *yea*).
34. yusŭ :        -        yu.
35.        ya ⎫
36.        ye ⎭ (only Cyrill.)
37. (ęn)        ę ⎫
38. (ąn)        ą ⎭ (nasal vowels).
39.        yę.
40.        yą.
41.        x (only Cyrill.)
42.        ps (only Cyrill.)
43.        th.
44.        ū.

The translation is given after Miklosich. The strange mixture of substantives, adverbs, and verbs, in different moods and tenses, indicates clearly that they must be corruptions of words not understood by the people, who tried to bring them nearer to their own understanding by the well-known process of popular etymology. They became *Slavonised*, if I may coin such a term.

This increased the perplexity, and thwarted every effort made to solve the problem ; but even greater was the difficulty with regard to the form.

It would be useless to summarise here all that has been said on this subject.

Professor Miklosich, with his usual thoroughness and mastery of his subject, has summed up the whole matter and given the entire bibliography.* His opinion, of course, is of the greatest weight. He proves the absolute dependence of the Cyrillitza upon the Glagolitza, and considers the latter to be the alphabet used by the apostles of the Slavonians themselves. In order to explain why they accepted such a complicated alphabet, Professor Miklosich suggests that it may have previously existed and been in use among the Slovenes, and that therefore Cyril and Method adopted it. "Nevertheless," says Professor Miklosich, "this alphabet is not a primitive and invented, but an *adopted* alphabet, taken over from somewhere else," without, however, giving us the slightest hint as to the alphabet from whence it was derived.

* Allgemeine Encyclopædie of Ersch und Gruber, vol. lxviii., 1859, pp. 403-422, *s. v.* Glagolitisch.

The decisive point of his utterance is that the Glagolitza is an alphabet originally destined for another language, and in later times adapted to the Slavonian.

From this point of view only can we explain the superfluous richness of signs observable in the enumeration above. They were necessary in the original, serving for the expression of some language very rich in sounds, and taken over entirely as it was, and adapted to the expression of the Slavonic alphabet, itself very rich, but not nearly so much so as the other.

This must be the starting-point of our inquiry. That many have endeavoured to ascertain the origin of the Glagolitza has already been mentioned. Professor Miklosich reviews these opinions, and his condemnation renders it unnecessary for us to reiterate them and refute them. But after the publication of that essay by Professor Miklosich there appeared two other attempts, with which I will now deal shortly.

The first is that of Mr. Taylor, who suggests that the Greek cursive alphabet and the combination of signs in the tachygraphical writing of the Greek might have served as a model for the Glagolitic. The comparison, however, shows such a complicated mode of passing from one into the other, that on formal grounds alone this idea must be rejected. To this may further be added the fact

that sounds like *sh, ch, j,* and others not existing
in the Greek could not be borrowed from these,
even not as combinations of letters. σχ retained for
ever its sound as σχ, and only nowadays do we de-
compose the combined sounds into their elements
by physiological inquiries into the nature of human
speech, a process unheard of in ancient times, when
for each *sound one simple* sign was used.

Not much better is the theory of Geitler, who
developed it in an elaborate and otherwise very
remarkable treatise.* He assumes that the strange
alphabet from which the Glagolitza is derived was
an old autochthonous Albanian alphabet, preserved
to the present time in a mutilated form in some
Albanian manuscripts. Not only the form of the
characters, but also their names are derived from
the Albanian. The first part has been thoroughly
annihilated by the profound criticism of Professor
Jagić ; † and as to the names, it will suffice to show
that some of them, considered by Geitler to be
Albanian, are *Turkish* elements of a very recent
origin, later than the fourteenth century, and therefore impossible to be of such an age as to be adopted
by Cyril in the eighth century, that is, six centuries
before. So, for instance, Albanian *meseletä,* from
which he derives Slavonic *myslete,* is plural of *mesel,*
Turkish, Arabic, and Hebrew *mashal* ; Albanian *lula*

---

* L. Geitler, Die Albanesischen und Slavischen Schriften, Wien, 1883.
† Archiv für Slav. Philologie.

is the Turkish *luleh*, pipe, with the same meaning, and has nothing whatsoever to do with *lyudye*, &c.*

Once agreed upon that point, that the Glagolitza is taken from another people, my view is that we must seek to find at the time when Cyril flourished such an alphabet, rich in sounds and not so far distant, that it could not easily be reached or known by Cyril.

Some, induced by an apparent similarity between the Glagolitic *sh* and *ge* with the Coptic, sought the origin in the latter; but, in addition to the difficulty of proving Cyril's acquaintance with the Coptic, there is, moreover, no further similarity among all the remainder, consisting of thirty-eight signs. This view may therefore be disregarded. The *Latin* and *Greek*, through the scantiness of sounds, and therefore of signs and difference of form and order, also need not be brought under consideration, and it is quite another direction to which I turn in order to find the probable prototype of the Glagolitza.

Nobody has up till now taken into consideration the *Armenian* alphabet and the other kindred alphabet of *Georgia*, so rich in sounds and signs, that they are unequalled and unsurpassed by any others.

*The relationship and dependence of the Glagolitza upon this or another alphabet akin to it of*

* v. Geitler, *l. c.*, pp. 168–171.

*those regions is now for me beyond any doubt,*
and I will endeavour to prove it in the following
pages.

Let us first examine the historical conditions and
establish the connection between Cyril and these
alphabets.

As it has been said above (p. 136), Cyril was
brought up at the court of Constantinople, receiv-
ing the best education, and his knowledge of Eastern
languages was especially praised. One of the most
important Eastern languages of the time was the
Armenian, the language of a rich literature and a
powerful Church, often mixed up with ecclesiastical
disputes, and playing an important *rôle* in the
history of Manichæism. It is further noteworthy
that the Armenians sent emissaries everywhere
challenging the orthodox, and the halls of the
palace in Byzantium resounded often enough with
their speeches and disputes.

There is no doubt that Cyril, the learned monk,
who himself was sent later on as an emissary to
the Khazars, and who took part at the conversion
of the Pannonian Slavonians, must have known
this language, spoken at the gates of Constantinople.

It is no matter of consequence to ask now the
origin of the Armenian alphabet itself, but even
the history of this invention is so striking an
analogy to the history of the Glagolitza, that it is

worth while to mention it here briefly, the more
so as it also explains the apparent similarity between Coptic and Glagolitic characters.

All the native writers are unanimous in ascribing
the invention of the present Armenian alphabet to
the Bishop Mesrup (fifth century), who succeeded
by these means in freeing himself from the Greek
influence and establishing a genuine Armenian
Church and literature. He first translated the
Bible into the Armenian language, thus forming
the basis for the new literature.

There are now different views as to the question
of the model taken by Mesrup for his new alphabet.
I, for my own part, derive it in its essential parts,
against the opinion of Mr. F. Müller,* from the
Zendic alphabet of the neighbouring Persians, with
which the Armenians were avowedly well acquainted. One single glance suffices to show the
similarity between these two alphabets. But the
Zendic is poor in signs, as the Persian dialect has
not so many sounds, and this want had to be
supplied from other sources. The chief source
was here the *Coptic* alphabet. If we remember
that some of Mesrup's prominent pupils, Moses of
Chorene, the famous Armenian chronicler, and
others, spent a long time in Alexandria, then the
difficulty arising from the distance between Armenia and Egypt is easily removed. For they had

* Sitzungsberichte of the Academy of Vienna, vol. xlviii. pp. 431-438.

been sent by their master to collate the oldest Greek manuscripts of the Bible preserved in the great library of Alexandria, with their translation into Armenian. The only alphabet of a Christian people rich in signs, and thus serving their purpose, was the Coptic, and so they took from it the elements wanting to complete their own new alphabet.

From Armenia this alphabet spread to the North, and was soon adopted by the Georgians, who adapted it to their own requirements, also changing here and there the shape of the letters; for instead of being angular with sharp corners, they rounded the edges and added spirals and flourishes. This makes that alphabet somewhat more similar to the Glagolitza, also characterised by its spirals and flourishes.

The same alphabet no doubt also spread in South Russia, and most probably was known in the empire of the Khazars, at that time very powerful, and having a language—judging from the other Turko-Turanian languages to which this belonged —rich in both vowels and consonants.

It is at least remarkable to find in a peculiar Greek alphabet of Mariupol, discovered by the late Dr. Blau,* the characteristic letter *sh* represented in the same way as in the Armenian alphabet,

---

* Zeitschrift der Deutsch Morgenländischen Gesellschaft, vol. xxviii. pp. 562–576, and vol. xxix. 166–167.

which is the same as we have noted here in the Glagolitza, and hence in the Cyrillitza.

Our investigation would be much furthered if anything written in the *Khazaric* characters had been preserved, such as it was used by them in their proceedings. Unfortunately we have only, and this in a more modern copy, the *Hebrew* letter sent by the Khazars to Hisdai ibn Shaprut in Spain. Also of Khazaric origin, and this time genuine, I consider, is another Hebrew manuscript, recently discovered and described by Professor Harkavy, who does not, however, recognise its origin, and considers it, without any internal proof, to be from Crete. As it was a well-known alphabet, and a Biblical text, there was no need to introduce any different letter, as is the case when writing down, even with the same characters, other foreign words or names. It is therefore difficult to prove the influence of a genuine alphabet. Nevertheless, I think that, for instance, the peculiar flourished *m* can be traced only to such an influence, as it offers in the way of its upward spiral a striking resemblance to the Armenian and Georgian *m*.

What further induces me to see in this MS. a text written by a *Khazar* is that there is no difference made between *ch* (*cheth*) and *h* (*he*), unknown also to the Karaïms, who are surely remnants of the Khazars, and so forth.

If I have insisted especially upon this point, it

is because the life of Cyril is also intimately connected with the Khazars, as he was sent thither by
the Emperor to convert them to Christianity.

His biography describes with many details his
stay at the court, and the disputations he had there
with Jews and Mohammedans.

Here, no doubt, already more or less acquainted
with the Armenian, he came across another similar alphabet, and when he decided to compose a
special alphabet for his Slavonic translations, he
only adopted this alphabet as the most fitting for
its purpose. He followed also at the same time
the example given by Mesrup centuries before.
In this connection we can now explain the hitherto
unknown origin of the Glagolitic alphabet, and
we proceed to a minute examination to ascertain
how far the historical explanation is backed by
the similarity between the Glagolitza and an
alphabet closely resembling the Armenian and
Georgian.

If we now consider the *forty* signs of the Glagolitical alphabet in the annexed plates, we can easily
detach at least *seven* as composed from two other
primitive elements, thus reducing the total number
of signs to thirty-three. The composed are the
following :—No. 22, out of $17 + 30$; 26, of $29 + 21$;
31, of $30 + 10$; 38, of $17 + 37$; 39, of $11 + 37$ or
of $6 + 37$; 40, of $10 + 37$ or $30 + 37$ (Miklosich);
and, finally, 34, which seems to be composed of

30 + 17 ; this latter turned on one side. Nos. 30 and 32 seem originally to be identical, but we leave that for the moment unsettled. The elements of combination are the vowels *i, ĭ (ŭ), ǫ, ę,* forming the peculiar Slavonic *preyoted* vowels. No. 26 is simply composed of the two elements *sh − t.*

It is now noteworthy that the vowel *u* is formed of *o* and *u.* We have further two doublets, viz., Nos. 8 and 9, both representing a similar (*z*) sound, and Nos. 10 and 11, both *i.* In this alphabet there are also two signs for *o,* Nos. 17 and 25 ; and what is more curious, No. 24, when compared with No. 4, both *g,* although Miklosich admits a difference between the two sounds. All these peculiarities point clearly to a foreign origin, where the alphabet consisted of at least the same number of signs, and where none of these signs were doublets, each of them representing a distinct sound.

If we now examine the Armenian alphabet, we shall find it composed of *thirty-six* letters, out of which *three* represent peculiar Armenian sibilants, not to be met with in any other language, and not to be distinguished from three other sibilants, except by a stronger pronunciation. These are rightly considered to be doublets of *č, ž,* and *tz,* and therefore left out, and we have thus the exactly corresponding number of *thirty-three* letters, representing, as we shall soon see, the same sounds as the characters of the Glagolitza. The similarity also extends to the

| GLAGOLITIC (CYRILLIAN). | | | GEORGIAN. | | | ARMENIAN MODERN AND OLD PRONUNCIATION. | | |
|---|---|---|---|---|---|---|---|---|
| 1 | ⳑ ✝ | | α | Ⴑ ⴑ | | a | ⴹ | α | a |
| 2 | ⴄ (ⴂ) | | b | Ⴅ ⴂ | | b | ⴼ | b | p |
| 3 | ⴄ | | v | Ⴈ | | v (u) | ⴖ | v | u |
| 4 | ⴊ ⴋ | | g | Ⴒ | | g | ⴼ | g | k |
| 5 | ⴍ ⴑ | | d | Ⴒ | | d | ⴼ | d | t |
| 6 | ⴈ ⴈ | | e | Ⴋ | | ē | ⴇ | e | e |
| 7 | ⴊⴊ ⴊⴊ | | ž | ⴐ ⴈ | | dz | ⴑ | ž | ž |
| 8 | ⴔ ⴅ | | dz | ⴆ ⴈ | | z | ⴒ | dz | tz |
| 9 | ⴖ ⴖ | | z | ⴇ | | z | ⴎ | dz | tz |
| 10 | ⴂ ⴗ | | i | ⴈ ⴈ | | ě | | | |
| 11 | ⴐ ⴊ | | i | ⴈ | | ī | ⴁ | y | y |
| 12 | ⴗ ⴖ | | dy (g) | ⴑ (§γ̇ε̇) | | K' | ⴼ | g' | K' |
| 13 | ⴗ ⴗ | | K | ⴈ (5 Kh) | | K | ⴼ | x | x |
| 14 | ⴀ ⴀ | | l | | | | ⴿ | e | e |
| 15 | ⴖ | | m | ⴈ | | m | ⴆ | m | m |
| 16 | ⴗ | | n | | | | | | |
| 17 | ⴗ ⴗ | | o | ⴍ | | o | ⴖⴼ | ō | ō |
| 18 | ⴕ ⴕ | | p | | | | ⴘ | p | b |
| 19 | ⴑ ⴑ | | r | ⴔ | | r | ⴖ | z | z |
| 20 | ⴅ | | s | | | | ⴖ | s | s |
| 21 | ⴑ ⴑ | | t | ⴖ | | t | ⴈ | t | d |
| 22 | ⴗⴗ ⴗ | | ū (ou) | | | ū (ou) | ⴖⴼ | u | (ou) |

| GLAGOLITIC (CYRILLIAN). | GEORGIAN. | ARMENIAN MODERN AND OLD PRONUNCIATION. |
|---|---|---|

| | | | | | | | | |
|---|---|---|---|---|---|---|---|---|
| 23 | ⊕ | Ꝑ | f (ph) | Ꝑ | ph | Ꝑ | f | f |
| 24 | ⅃ | φ | h | ȝ | k̕ | ⌇ | hh | hh |
| 25 | ⊖ | φ | ō | | | ● | ō | ō |
| 26 | ш∞ | Ѱ | št | | | | | |
| 27 | v | (Ҹ) | tz | Ꝋ | tz | δ | tz | dž |
| 28 | ⅌ | (Ҹ) | č | Ꝝ | č' | Ȣ | dž | č |
| 29 | ш | | š | | | | | |
| 30 | Ꙗ ∕ (ъ.ь) | ŭ (ŭ) | ᕴ (ъ hae) hoe | | ⌈ | e̥ | e̥ |
| 31 | Ꙗ Ꞁ (ъ⅃) | ŭy | | | | | |
| 32 | Ꙗ (ь.ъ) | ĭ (ŭ) | ᕴ (ъ hae) hoe | | ⌈ | e̥̊ | e̥̊ |
| 33 | Ⰰ Ⰱ (Ꞁъ) | ê | ᔇ | y | ⌈ᴜ | ê | ê |
| 34 | Ꝓ Ⅲ (ꞁ) | yu | | (ᴫᴜ | yu yu) |
| 35 | | (ꞁꙗ) | yα | | | | | |
| 36 | | (ꞁᴇ) | ye | | | | | |
| 37 | ⅽ | Ꞁ | e | Ч | vĭé | | | |
| 38 | ⅼⅽ | ⁆ⅽ | α | | | | | |
| 39 | ⁆ⅽ | | ye | | | | | |
| 40 | ⲫⅰ | Ѳⅽ | ya | | | | | |
| 41 | | (𝒳) | h | | | | | |
| 42 | 🔲 | (𝝭) | ps | | | | | |
| 43 | ⌅ | (ϑ) | th | | | | | |
| 44 | 𝟅 | (ᴏꝩ) | ū (ou) | | | | | |

www.ingramcontent.com/pod-product-compliance
Lightning Source LLC
Chambersburg PA
CBHW020112030726
47498CB00006B/2068